I0825935

Boy in Blue Raincoat

This book is for my sons

Benjamin

&

Daniel

ISBN 9780648702740

Disclaimer: All materials in this publication are entirely the thoughts and the opinions of the writer Tom Law and do not reflect those of the publishers, producers or distributors. The author asserts that any likeness seemingly pertaining to any person or persons living or dead are purely coincidental and further, the publisher takes no responsibility for any such likenesses.

Published in Australia by:
Longership Publishing Australia
PO Box 71 Swifts Creek Victoria 3896
AUSTRALIA
ABN 73446736413
email: longership@email.com

First published in Australia 2011
This 2nd Edition: November 2020
Cover design and sketches: Tom Law
The right of Tom Law to be identified as the Author of the Work has been asserted in accordance with the Copyright, Designs and Patents Act 1988.

Law, Tom 1945-
Boy in Blue Raincoat
ISBN: 9780648702740
pp 136

boy in

blue raincoat

Tom Law

Longership Publishing Australia

Contents

Mill

Ah Fat

Newcomer

Goldmine

School

Revelry

Soldier

Trust

Shearing

Mountain

Stream

Family

Confusion

Sea

Community

Doubt

'The Boy'

Mill

For the boy the world was large. For the world, the world of the boy was a fishbowl. But it was sufficient. The boy's understanding of his micro environ was complete with enough room for further exploration or merely the joy of familiar ground. He was sometimes introvert and melancholy; at play-acting, in his element. He feared not to be alone as long as he was bathed in the rich tapestry of the forest gulley and within earshot of its gurgling stream. The chattering of parakeets and arrhythmic symphony of bellbirds, thrushes, wrens and other small birds held his mind and brought both joy and an inner glow. This was *his* world and where *he* belonged.

4.30 am and the families in mill row are stirring. It is a rimy spring morning and the air is crisp and still. By 5.30 most of the machinery is humming and whirring as the men commence their daily work of flitching, rough sawing, docking and planing. Smoke rises from the cone where sawdust and scraps are burned. The odours of eucalypt, diesel and smoke mingle but the strongest scent of all comes from the drying kilns, a soft woody smell. Many of the men roll their own tobacco and smoke whilst at their job. Concentration is absolute if they wish to avoid an accident, so common at timber mills.

"Coming to the meet at ten Tom?" a burly man with long dark hair and dark unshaved face calls across the noisy yard.

"Sure thing but can't seem to persuade Mitch here… he seems happy enough with no shithouse doors in the loo!"

"It's not as though there's any women prowling around" retorts Mitch with a hint of a smile creeping across his ginger bearded face. The wrinkles across his forehead lift to form deep furrows. Mitch has been on the team for twenty years now.

"That's not the point… this fudging useless union wouldn't frighten Miss Muffet away or even ask for shithouse paper its so frigging weak!"

The mill hands often talked that way to each other. Mostly they were married men with families and were tough but generous folk. Many had worked on the Black Spur or down on the west coast of Tasmania, following the life of the timber mill worker as best one could. The pay wasn't much unless you worked a lot of overtime at weekends. But basic housing was provided and at least some insurance against the worst event such as losing a hand, finger or the like.

It was 7.30 now and the boy's mother called to him that he must rise and wash if he did not wish to be late for school. Sleepily he entered the kitchen and helped himself to a piece of cold toast and vegemite still lying on the pink fake marble tabletop. He smeared the butter on well and thickly.

"Get yerself inta the shower and get dressed first yer scoundrel. I'll fix you some fry up.. now get!" his mum said sternly. The boy sauntered out at his own pace, still clutching his unfinished morsel. Just then the emergency siren howled through the town, reflecting from the blue-grey and ochre hills, screeching panic and fear into the hearts of the mill folk. A young man with long golden locks to his shoulders came running to the back door. Mrs MacIntyre immediately read the expression on his face and the quiver in his voice.

"Its Dan Mrs Mack, you'd better come quick!"

The mother of three tore off her apron and followed the apprentice out the back gate, across the yard to the docking area. Her husband sat quietly, a corn coloured hessian sack clutched against his right shoulder. Several men were tightly huddled. The manager arriving at about the same time called to the man "How is it Dan?"

Timber Mill at Rushing Creek

But the man just sat there with glazed eyes, staring straight ahead. He was aware of nothing and gave no response to his wife Mary. She looked at him as if for the first time, seeing a thin lean man in his mid thirties but looking like a sufferer from a concentration camp. He had beads of sweat on his brow; his face unshaven and ashen. Mitch pressed a lighted rolly between his lips.

"Suck on this Dan, the ambulance is on its way mate. You'll be right in a jiff'.

There was a lot of blood. Dan's arm was wrapped in some newspaper and lay on a neatly piled stack of freshly cut 'four be twos', the timber smelling fresh in the morning sun. It had been severed cleanly just below the elbow. Mary gave out a little scream and promptly fainted in cataplexy. One of the younger men walked away and could barely stand from the sight of the blood… so much blood!

The boy eventually came back to the kitchen. "Mum" he called. But only his younger brother sat at the table and his baby sister was still strapped in her highchair.

"Mummy gone to mill" was all his brother could say. He was intent on watching a cartoon on a small TV screen. The boy made himself some more toast, smeared a generous helping of strawberry jam on it and sidled out the back door, making his way around the house under the shade of ancient plane trees that lined the highway through the village. School was just two hundred metres away on the other side of the road. He was just fourteen and this morning he would be early for a change.

He made his way to the school crossing and hurried across to the school gate. There were a few girls laughing and chatting together as he passed.

“Morning Macky, wanna kiss me?” one of the girls taunted. But the boy took this as a compliment, smiled and passed along. He ventured beyond the red brick main building then on towards the grassy oval at the rear. A group of boys from his class were huddled between two shabby portable classrooms sharing a cigarette.

“Hey Macky, stay there an’ keep yer eyes peeled for ol’ man Jacobs. ‘eez on duty this morning.” Another boy approached nervously “Macky, de yer know who’s got hurt at the mill? Me da’s working today an’ we’ve heard nothing yet.”

The boy shook his head, hands in pockets and absently kicking at stubble on the ground.

“Heard the siren, that’s all!” The boys went back to their smoking and teenage argot.

The boy now focussed on some others kicking a footy to each other on the oval. There were still patches of frost in the shade of the old manna gums fringing the oval and between the portables where he stood. He was in some far away world of his own when he heard the teacher’s voice.

“MacIntyre, your dad has been in an accident at the mill, you’d better come along with me to the office. And I want to see you three at morning recess!” he said to the other boys more sternly.

The other boys were cursing the boy for not doing his guard duty but at the same time could tell that his father had most likely had a serious injury. There was nothing they could do. They were caught and would just have to cop their punishment.

The boy’s father would be off work for a few months. There would be the insurance but it would likely take up to a year before being paid out. Nevertheless he had the mill house as basic as it was and Dan could spend some time with the boy. He would still receive his basic pay but without overtime the family would have to live frugally. Rushing Creek was a friendly and small village of some four hundred souls. A mix of farmers, timber mill workers, forest workers, Forest Commission and State Electricity employees. A pub, a post-office, a Bush Nurse Centre, a café, a general store and a garage cum repair shop. Three churches vied for the spiritual hearts of the community: Anglican, Catholic and Uniting. A primary and secondary school, fire-engine, police station with one permanently residing constable together with his family, a bakery, a butcher shop, road transport and cartage centre, a small motel, the recreation hall, the football oval, tennis courts and bowling green. A caravan-park and camping ground adjacent to the river, a rifle range and a golf course at some distance complemented the small but active community. Nestled on a large river plain and surrounded by distant forested hills with farming land closer in, the village was a most picturesque and delightful place. It was mostly sunny all the year round with a minimal rainfall of 635 mm of rain per annum. Winter nights were frosty but quickly faded to bright crisp days with clear blue skies. Snow would appear on the surrounding hills but a fall in the village perhaps on a single day every three years or so. Beef, mutton, lamb and wool were the mainstays of the farming community but hardwood timber the lifeblood of the village. Tourism played a fairly minor role. The timber mill produced scantling and frame timbers for the building trade in Melbourne. However, flooring and some panelling were also produced. Messmate and mountain ash were highly sought after. Over the first half of the twentieth century there was an abundant supply in the region of the Shire despite the 1939 fires. There were four hamlets in the area with a combined total population of barely two thousand people. Each had a timber mill excepting Rushing Creek that boasted two, one in the town and one, albeit considerably smaller, some five kilometres out of town on the Castle Road.

“Dan was always so careful on that machine, he never let a limb get too close to the blade” piped the Russian, “Anyone see what happened?” The men were deliberating over their sandwiches and coffee.

“I think a noggin was at the side an’ he was trying to flip it out with a slither of scantling” said Mitch.

“Yeah, well I worked on her for ten flaming years an’ she could be a temperamental bitch. Yer had te be watching every second” said Macalister, an old hand that had been there longer than anyone could remember.

“I know Dan was worried about his brother over Dargo way. He has some money worries an’ our Dan was going to give him a loan. Maybe it was on his mind this morning” said a younger man smoking a pipe.

“That’s ‘xactly it” piped in Macalister, his jacket, boots and trousers well worn and grubby. “Yer just can’t have anyting on yer mind working that fricking bitch ‘o machine. ‘bout time she was replaced wid summing safer by God!”

When the union rep discussed the doors for the toilets later that day with the management, there was no argument or discussion. This was unusual. But there was a heightened tension after the accident and it was really a small concession.

“Not a problem, we’ll see to it right away”.

Being a Friday, many of the men converged on the rambling pub on the corner of the main crossroad at the centre of the town, the Old Dover. The aristocrats (wealthier graziers) had their personal corner of the bar whilst the farm hands, government workers, tree fallers and mill workers crowded in. Schoolies, itinerants and the odd tourist made up

Friday Night- Old Dover Pub

the complement to a rowdy crowded bar smelling of sweat and tobacco. The Old Dover was a timber framed building with hardwood planking, flooring, panelling all painted on the outside to a cream and green motif. The roofing was traditional iron having withstood sun, sleet and wind for a hundred years. The bar area was large. A smaller lounge existed with neat dark brown wood panelling together with a largish dining hall and kitchen. The main hallway, windowless and with the same panelling was dark, leading to various rooms for travellers and one or two permanent residents. There was a very large outdoor area at the rear which was not used for patrons at this time but the ancient palm tree begged of an earlier period of grandiose indulgence when gold ran freely in men's pockets. Of course the talk was mainly about Dan's bad luck that day. It was another week to pay day and a hat went around "for the missus to get in a few extras for the kids and that!" so the giant of a man said as he passed among the drinkers. The publican Jim MacNamara, a portly man of Irish descent in his late sixties, pulled a fat bundle of notes from his pocket, peeled off a hundred and dropped it into the hat. He was that sort of a chap. Ran a good pub with basic but appetising fare at reasonable prices and with a generous heart.

"Tell Mrs Mack if there's anything I can do for her she just has to let me know" he said in plain speech.

Usually by eight, many would have returned home to wives and families or removed to the dining room for dinner. But this night the men of the town seemed not to want to go home and the beer flowed way past ten o'clock closing. Fortunately for most, their homes were just a short stagger away.

The next morning across the road, there lay Jonny Patel, the town drunk. He lay calmly sleeping with a large sack of supplies and beer bottles at his side, all covered in frost. The local cop gave him a nudge. "Seven already Jonny, you'd best be up and on your way!"

Without any more than an almost imperceptible grunt, Jonny was up on his feet and walking up the Castle Road twitching his head at an angle and looking up at the trees and flitting birds with a cheerful if not distorted smile. A few kilometres along the road he started to sing over and over "Rocky Mountain High in Colorado… " He was a very large swarthy man of part Indian origin and worked seasonally in the shearing sheds around the district. But he liked his grog! He sang as the magpies and noisy miners swooped down at is head. Seven kilometres along he arrived at his shanty near the creek on a small triangular patch of perhaps a half acre adjacent to two ramshackle timber dwellings. It was a serene little paradise for a loner. He lit an outside campfire and started to boil a billycan for a drink of tea, all the while continuing to sing the chorus line of the John Denver classic. Blue smoke rose uninterrupted to the sky near to where a tipsy caravan huddles close to a leaning iron shed, all beneath a backdrop of a dark and steeply rising forest. Nearby, another mill worker was ploughing an acre of ground with a Clydesdale and traditional wood and iron hand-held plough with the hope of planting potatoes before the weekend was out. Blue wrens followed and pecked at the worms and insects on the freshly turned earth as the complaisant draught horse furrowed over the stony ground. A kookaburra sat patiently on a branch of an ancient forest red gum. The small stream hummed and chattered softly as dragonflies hovered and a zephyr tickled the tops of reeds along its course. The day was indeed pleasant.

He was born in the summer of his twenty seventh year
Coming home to a place he'd never been before
He left yesterday behind him, you might say he was born again
You might say he found a key for every door
When he first came to the mountains his life was far away
On the road and hanging by a song
But the string's already broken and he doesn't really care
It keeps changing fast and it don't last for long……

Rocky Mountain High- John Denver

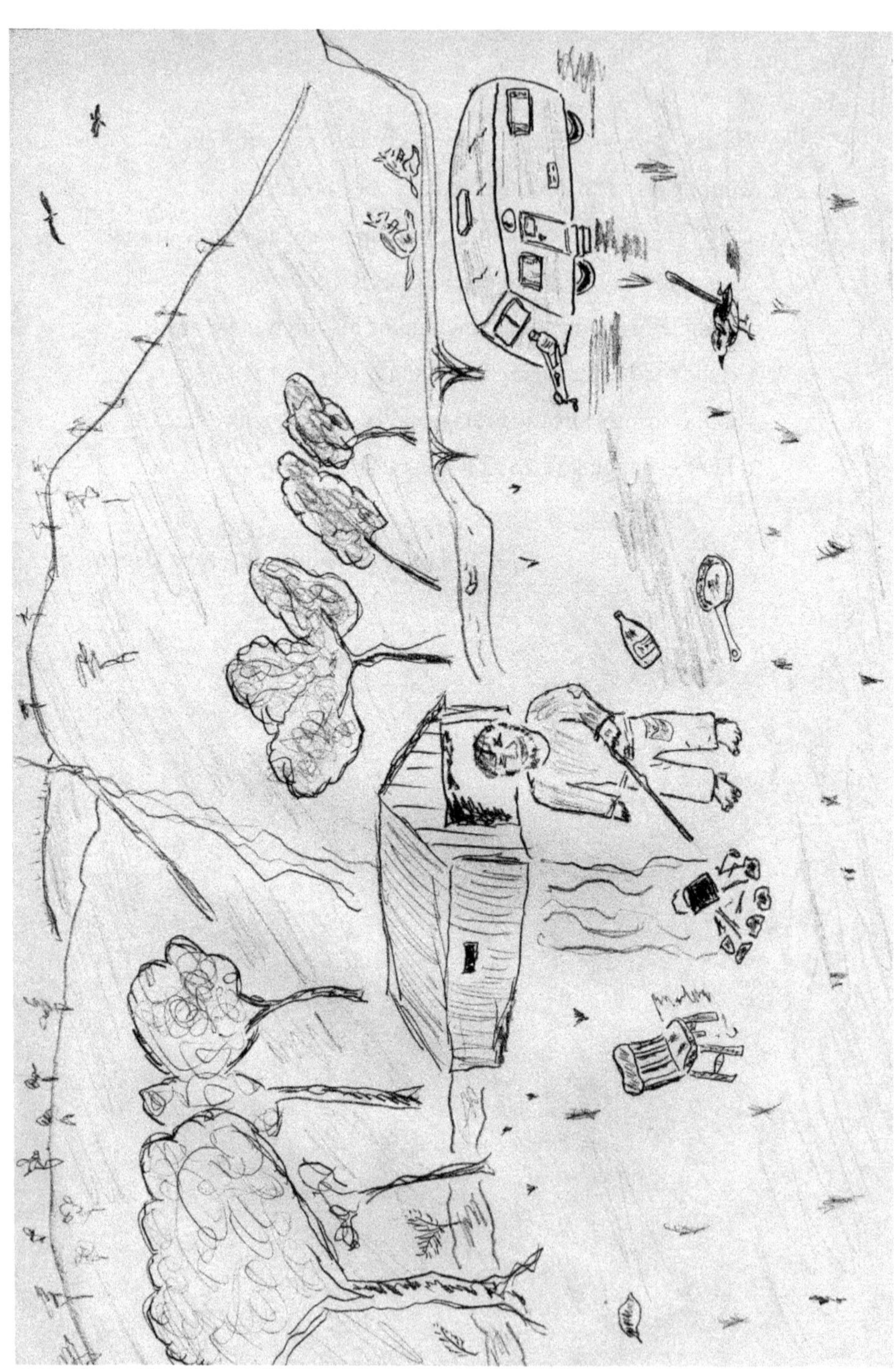

Jonny Patel....   "Rocky mountain high in Colorado ...."

Ah Fat

It was during the early 1850's that the young Chinese man Fat Yi Hao worked very hard as a farm labourer for his Lord just 80 miles North West of Nangking near the hamlet of Xuyi. Nanking was the seat of the ancient Wu kingdom. It was Fu Chai, Lord of the State of Wu that founded a fort named Yecheng 冶城 in the Nanking area in 495 BC according to legend. The city has experienced destruction and renewal many times. Nanking first became a capital in 229 AD, under Sun Quan of the Wu Kingdom during the Three Kingdoms Period. But the writer wanders.

Fat Yi Hao lived in a small hut of river stones with thatched straw roof and shared with his mother, sister Fu Lu and younger brother Fei Wu. They had a few chickens, some ducks and two milking goats. The family were allowed to raise vegetables on a small allotment 20 feet by 40 feet. Most spring through summer, summer through autumn, this small tendered patch of black soil yielded sufficient for them to live upon. The nearby large lake, its streams and tributaries provided the family with good fish. The small amount of brass coin that Yi Hao earned supplemented this, enabling the purchase of material and tools for the mother to make clothes for them all. But occasionally the winters were harsh and long with much snow. Late planting and cultivation brought hunger to their bellies. When the younger brother was of age to work for the Lord, Yi Hao decided to travel and look for a better way of life. He had heard of gold being found in America on the Yukon. Some said there was new gold being found in Australia. His mother and sister wept when he made up his mind to travel out of China and escape the hegemony of Lords and aristocrats that possessed the land. He was just eighteen years when he left. Visiting the small temple in his village he lit incense, laid gifts of fruit and coins and prayed. He visited the mound under which his father lay and prayed again. Looking across the flat damp landscape he espied men and women working the patchwork of paddies, planting new rice seedlings or ploughing with ox and wood. He sat for a long time speaking to his revered and much loved father. Looking across to the fishponds he watched a group of ducks rise from the tall reeds. He let out a small sigh then returned to the hut. Finally, he went round to each house and bade farewell to his friends and neighbours. Not looking back and with moist eyes he trudged southwards along the ochre dirt track. Unknowingly, he was never to return to his birthplace and native home, his brother Fei Wu now becoming the pater familias!

Slowly working his way to Nanking, he diverted his attention to its ancient walls, palace and temples before moving on to Shanghai. Here, Yi Hao found a place on a local trading vessel bound for Hong Kong. On reaching there, he paid his passage and embarked onto a British sailing trader bound for Port Adelaide and Robe, South Australia in the new colony. By landing in the free port of Robe and travelling over the unguarded Victorian border the gold seeker was able to evade the Victorian Government's tax of £20 per Chinese. It was in February 1856 that the ship 'Sumatra' under Captain Grievel sailed from Hong Kong where nearly four hundred fellow Chinese, mainly from Canton (Guangzhou) joined. The young man was no sailor and succumbed to nausea for much of the voyage but he survived. Unfortunately there were several deaths among his fellow Chinese before the ship reached South Australia.

It was in late June of the same year that Ah Fat (the name his fellow Cantonese now preferred) commenced walking to the goldfields at Bendigo, a journey of some 300 miles. Thousands of Chinese poured onto the goldfields at this time, mainly from Canton. However, by mistake, Ah Fat followed a small group of his associates along the route to the Ovens valley, some 500 miles from his point of disembarkation. White farmers and native blacks alike watched in amazement the long line of yellow men with their distinctive broad woven bamboo hats, loose cotton trousers with over-smock and on their shoulder a bamboo pole upon which they carried all their worldly goods tied in a square of canvass.

It is said that by 1859 the number of Chinese in Victoria passed 40,000 and made up nearly 20 per cent of the adult male population in the colony.

Racial hostility led to riots on the Buckland goldfields in Victoria in 1857. At the Buckland River in North East Victoria early in July 1857 (just a year after Ah Fat had arrived there), riots followed a rumour about the unnatural behaviour of a Chinese man. The rumour was seen as proof that the Chinese were less human whom practised abominations and made lewd gestures towards white women. None was true. The only truth was the jealousy of some white miners at the successes of the Chinese miners.

In July 1857, white miners called a meeting at the Buckland where the leaders called on their fellow diggers to take the law into their own hands and drive the Chinese out. Men on horseback armed with bludgeons, sticks and whips charged the Chinese, destroying their encampment of tents and stores. In retreat, they were forced to cross the river via a single log bridge. Two and a half thousand Chinese were driven off the Buckland and were it not for a handful of armed English miners who protected the Chinese from the vicious melee, many might have died.

Ah Fat and a few close friends decided to take an arduous track over the mountains to find the fledgling thorp of Battery where a new find was rumoured. It was difficult going in extreme cold conditions with patches of snow on the mountain tops. But after six days they made it and were joined by many other Chinese over the ensuing years. Here they worked for ten years on the Livingstone Creek panning and sluicing for the fine alluvial gold. They would scour the land for signs of a quartz reef, even using a green willow twig as dowser for the metal. Later they moved down to Castle and Munjie West and worked over old ground along the Rushing Creek. For a period, Ah Fat worked on the new findings of alluvial on the Ghost Stream. It was here in this charmed retreat that he started to take note of the trees and various birds particularly the thrushes, robins, the profusion of lorikeets, rosellas and parrots of such diverse flash and colour. His native home gradually slipped from his mind as he felt one with his new home.

Ah Fat had made a little money and decided he would try his hand at market gardening. He returned to the upper Rushing Creek near the growing hamlet of Munjie West and took up a handful of acres on a broad flat. This was a remote spot and he made reasonable money from the miners by selling water melon and a range of much wanted fresh vegetables. Some miners even paid him with a few grains of the yellow metal in lieu of cash. He built a primitive one roomed log hut with a stone chimney in the side of a hill just a mile below the new town and being across the stream from that area known as the Gum Forest. Close by his hut he tilled the deep soil by hand tools and sowed regenerated seeds from a variety of vegetables. He had no woman but neither was he a misogynist, being sufficiently content with his small paradise and his bird friends that he conversed with every day. Winters brought heavy frosts and the occasional sprinkling of snow. Summers were sometimes so dry that the small creek dried up and he need cart water from a distant pool. He would travel to Maintown once each two years to purchase seeds, provisions and simple tools. Although only eighty miles away, the journey was an arduous task along a narrow dirt road. He would travel by open wagon and be away for over a week on these occasions. On one visit he acquired a small and rare magnolia cutting of Soulangiana- the Chinese magnolia tree and a Japanese cherry seedling from a Chinese merchant. He planted this grandiflora magnolia on a small rise close to the stream and the cherry behind his humble abode. It gave him pleasure to tender these and experience the burst of fragrant flowers and blossom at the herald of each spring, particularly the large pink, white and purple cups of the magnolia.

The tawny frogmouths, wedge tailed eagles and tiny blue wrens were his companions by day. At night the haunting boobooks lulled him to slumber under a million shimmering points of light in a sparkly sky.

Ah Fat lived a solitary life until laid to rest at the Castle cemetery in 1912 where he sleeps still alongside many of his fellow Chinese in unmarked graves. But it is a quiet and peaceful place. The bustle of mining is gone and the thousands that travelled over the bush in search of the yellow metal are departed also. The dreams of men are transitory and are soon dissipated into the eternity of time. The stars and mountains, forests and streams are troubled no more. The ring of the miners' steel pick and hammer silenced as natures peculiar sounds enrich the breezes playfully rolling through the gullies and woods. The bellbirds and whipbirds compete with the soft gurgle of the singing brook. Blackwoods struggle to regain their ground. For a time at least, all is as it should be over this distant landscape of blue grey hills and darkened gullies whilst men are called away to distant wars. The land awaits calmly for the woodcutters and newcomers of a new and future generation. Ah Fat's hut is now no more than a pile of stones once forming his cosy hearth beneath an aged and drooping flowering plum tree. The bush slowly but surely encroaches over the purple and ochre mispickel of tailings' mounds. A huddle of satin bower birds along with their dominant shiny dark blue cock peck at the windfalls under the few trees in the dilapidated apple grove. But soon the softer sounds of building will ring across the stream as a new family takes a hold on this acreage. Children's peels of laughter will pierce the zephyrs tickling the willows, river gums and wattles as they play at the waters edge. Not a coda, but a whole new movement to the continuous symphony of life and nature as well as man's tempering and reshaping of his habitat; this time not as a conqueror but rather as a harmonious joining and fusion with a discerning respect for all that is already present in the environment.

Ah Fat hut

Newcomer

It had rained during the night and all was wet. Sun rays burst through the tree clad crest of the opposite hill to give narrow shafts of light through the rising mist. A black wallaby foraged close by as the boy pushed through the long wet grass, fern, nettle and thistle, flicking back sprays of jewels as their heads and stems sprang to their former upright positions. Broken black bark peeled from dead wattle. The lush and shady leaves of the tight foliage of blackwoods still provided an eerie shade twixt night and day. The creek gurgled and sang as it meandered between rounded boulders. The boy wore rubber boots and his blue raincoat. He pressed against some dogwood and stumbled up a slippery pathway a few metres until he stood on a verdant river flat of just an acre or so. Turquoise, verte, olive, ochre.. every hue and shade of blue and green enveloped the boy. The gullies on distant hills still shrouded with fogs lay dark and black as they creased the spectre of hill folded behind hill and onward down the tight valley. The mingled verse of lorikeet, thrush, blue wren and bellbird played on his ears. Startled and perceiving a change he moved forward with evoked inquisitiveness. There were neatly piled stacks of timber covered in black plastic the skirts of which flapped about in the soft breeze. Low stone walls appeared forming a rectangle with a half-finished chimney standing clear at one end. Three large boxes of blue-grey slates randomly lay on the ground tilting this way and that. Each bore the label 'Devonian Quarries, Marysville'. Tethered, a large black goat stood aloft one of the boxes and gave a gentle bleat. A few tools lay scattered about such as hammers, shovels and steel wedges all bathed in a film of dew not yet dried.

The sun made more effort now, breaking the puffy clouds above and revealing an expanse of blue sky promising a fine day. Kookaburras laughed in unison in a gay chorus to welcome the morn. Many other birds were hopping hither, flying thither and filling the air with sweet melodies. The boy was taken aback at the new scene since his last visit to this cranny some months before. Suddenly the newcomer emerged from the doorway of a large steel shed tucked in close to the hill. Tall and slender grey box and apple box trees lurched menacingly above threatening its imminent destruction. Cascades of mistletoe, its fake leaves glittering red-orange reflecting the sunlight from their oily surfaces hung overhead. The newcomer wore a white grubby jumper with roll-neck and wine coloured chord jeans frayed at the knees. His long mane was of pure gold and his beard red and profuse as a pirate's. He stretched and yawned then his gaze fell upon the boy.

"Morning me lad, what's your game then so early?"

The boy was rooted and dumbfounded, not able to form words at all. In fear of the newcomer's countenance he just stared at the ground in front of him. In a gentler tone:

"Where did you come from? Did you walk all the way from town?"

The newcomer seemed friendly enough and the boy stammered:

"I often comes this way mister, for fishin' eels in the creek. I likes to poke about the dumps jest looking fer things you know".

"I see" said the newcomer "but it's so early in the day for a lad to be wandering the bush alone- you know these parts then?"

"Oh yes sir, I've been many times with me dad. But now I comes by meself mainly as dad is always busy workin'".

A robin flew onto the cement mixer, poised, looked about then flew down to pick up a grub then immediately flew away again. Picking up courage and surveying the scene the boy said:

"What are you doing here mister, building someint?"

"Yeah, it's a long project but I am building a house here. I hope you don't mind?" At this the boy shuffled his boots and looked down at the ground again. Without eye contact he just whispered:

“Its OK mister”.
“Call by any time then” said the newcomer as he started to shovel gravel and sand into the gaping mouth of the mixer. The boy gave a bit of a smile then retraced his steps back to the creek. The newcomer leant on his shovel watching the blue of the boy’s coat as it merged with the surrounding plants and trees until it disappeared altogether. A group of black cockatoos screeched as they swooped overhead, settling in the higher branches of the tall river gums.
“Omen of storms” thought the stranger at his self-constructed myth. “They’ve flown from the Dargo no doubts”.
The lad of hardly a baker dozen years or more slipped away along the stream, dazed as a sleepwalker. Then ‘cross pebble and brook investigating every corner for colour and living things to please his mind and tender his soul in harmony. ‘twas here he belonged; this his playground of nature’s gifts bestowed by that unseen cosmic hand for boy and man to wander or therein build his home at leisure; to explore, to engage and supplement the yearning inner soul.
He was certain that the boy was close at hand on many occasions after that. The newcomer sensed his presence in some way. But the boy, guarded, always kept his distance as he passed the building site so that the newcomer did not catch a glimpse of him again. However, on inquiring at the general store the newcomer gleaned a little of this solitary personage. He was the son of a mill hand.
“You know, the bloke who lost his arm a while back… that’s his eldest boy. He’s a MacIntyre!”
The newcomer also sensed that he had ventured into the boy’s world of escape on purchasing this wild three acre block adjacent to the old mine workings upon which to build a home for his young family. But the land was large and there was enough space for the boy to wander and fossick to his hearts content. The newcomer hoped the boy would

The newcomer meets the boy

remain happy and share without malice this small area of his playground.

Later that morning the newcomer and his young family were scouring hills and dales for the gifts of nature; namely mushrooms, mint and wild asparagus. Later in the season they will collect blackberries and later again, rosehips. But the most tedious of their efforts is the collecting of rocks and river stones for the walls of the new abode. Schist, granite and the occasional white quartz were all to be had close at hand. The miner's middens from their excavations in search of gold-bearing quartz reefs were everywhere and although often covered in moss and lichen, made easy pickings. The elder boy lets out a scream as he is bitten by a jumping jack and his mother comforts him with the immediate application of a soothing cream to the skin.

"You can continue alone now; we will return to the shed and I will prepare some lunch."

The young man with his shoulder length locks continues to place rocks into the small trailer pulled by a red super-bug (German VW car). He flicks off any unwanted ants, spiders or scorpions with a robotic dextrous swift movement of his hand. He has done such collecting so many times before it is now a natural rhythm and regimented process. When satisfied that the trailer is reasonably full, he drives back to the house-site and deposits the rocks on a growing pile.

The occasional copper head, black snake or large brown may be seen. There are no tiger snakes down here but plenty up in the higher country. A large blue tongue lizard lazily sleeps in the sun not caring on the activity close at hand. It is hot now and the cicadas drum to a deafening music in the trees above. It is a relief to enter the shed for respite of the day's heat and to peck at some delicacies prepared by the loving hand of his wife.

"Cold roast lamb, tomato and green chutney sangers… would you like tea or coffee?"

"I think I'll take a glass of milk.. might have a nap after lunch, too bloody hot to go out there!"

"Oh I forgot to mention that Guy Italiano is down the block unloading some hives. He said that you'd already OK'd it with him."

"Yeah, he promised to give us some honey. I'll stroll down as soon as I've finished eating."

"Oooh can I come too dad?" piped in young Bill.

"Well as long as you keep well clear and run home as soon as I tell you OK?"

"Great dad.. I will"

Although only a three year old, Bill would never wish to miss an opportunity of accompanying his dad on a stroll through the bush; and to see the bee-man at work was an extra bonus. Guy had travelled up from Romano Island on the Gippsland Lakes. He was familiar with the best places in the forested hinterland to place his bees and cautiously followed the seasonal burst of flowers from field, water course and gum tree to maximise the yield.

There was always such a variety of fare in the country kitchen. Quince jelly, rabbit pie, home made bread with the addition of walnuts, chestnuts, almonds and hazel nuts when in season. Guy's clover and wattle blossom honey was as clear as a mountain stream with the most delicate and fragrant aroma and taste… an elixir of the Gods! With the arrival of the first frost, the sweet texture of the perfumed persimmon was a breakfast favourite. The newcomer liked to make cider, blackberry nip, beers and other concoctions from the fruit at hand. A favourite was rosehip mead; tedious to make but a rewarding drink.

Heavy rain brought the Bogong moths from the ground. They flapped everywhere day and night for several days leaving their powdery trails over clothes and furniture, pillows and towels. The writer will regale with his story about a local farming lad that was called up to Geelong for a classy wedding of a former school chum. Retrieving his moth-balled suit from the wardrobe, off he went to the salubrious occasion, stuffing his prepared speech into his breast pocket. At the quintessential moment he stood with glass raised and pulled his sheet from the pocket. To the amazement and mirth of the guests, a giant Bogong moth emerged from same pocket and flapped over table among the now hysterical revellers.

"Well Bruce" retorted the groom spontaneously, "you've certainly brought the Snowy Mountains to Geelong!"

The newcomer was very busy over the next week preparing for the 'raising'. There were twelve massive messmate beams lying close to the stone walls of lounge and kitchen, now completed to ten feet or so from the ground. Each beam was about sixteen feet in length and six inches by twelve inches in cross-section. These must be raised to straddle the stone walls and being several hundred weight each, some thought and careful planning on the operation was necessary.

After playing with his son's Fischertechnik, the newcomer devised a hoist in the form of two parallelogram structures pivoted on large bolts acting as axles. With the aid of steel cable, block pulleys and a friend's 4-wheel drive vehicle, the beams could be lifted horizontally and slid across the walls into position. The big day arrived and a dozen friends assembled to assist with lifting and cheering. Remarkably the job was completed in less than two hours. Glazed Dave exclaimed "I just wish my father was here to see this!" Soon after, wives and children joined for a picnic and celebration with much food, wines and beers and home-made lemon cordial. The story swapping on the progress of each of the other owner-builders was intense. Then topics such as brewing, tree-planting and vegetable growing were taken up with keen interest. Seed savers were discussed as well as different approaches to tilling and preparing the soil for various crops. The scene reminded one of the Christian Germanic Amish people of America. This was a community effort extraordinaire and much appreciated by the newcomer and his family. The way was now prepared for the raising of ridge and rafters which the newcomer would do mainly by his self with a little assistance from the Russian.

Later that evening there was to be a 'Bush Dance' at the Mechanics Institute in Rushing Creek. Most representatives of the new influx of owner builders and their families were there along with many local families. The band 'The Rollickin Bushwhackers' up from Stratford way included a variety of traditional instruments including Gaelic tabors, bodhrans and flutes. The mix of music was of Celtic renaissance, traditional Australian and American country folk. The Pride of Erin and many progressive square dances were taught to the novices by the eloquent gestures and guidance of the band's compare and leader, one Max Guilgrig.

It was a wonderful evening of ancient pageantry where adults and children mixed freely on the dance floor to pass away the evening having immense fun. It mattered not if you were novice or expert. Everyone passed a delightful and friendly evening to the beat of simple and uncomplicated music. The band members were shared among the guests for free lodging. In one case, the music continued at home to the wee small hours accompanied by non-conservative quantities of liqueurs and rolled tobacco.

The night demonstrated a welcomed tolerance of the established country folk to the idealistic young invaders from the city. At last one could detect a melding of the two with meaningful dialogue and learning on both sides. There were no extreme puritanical stances but an appreciation to the views of each. For the country folk, some of their long held views were challenged. For the idealists from the big smoke, the recognition that country life is not so simple or easy came as a shock. But they were hardy stock and took each blow in their stride and loved every moment of their chosen pathways. All had slightly different approaches, but all made up a beautiful patchwork of a new society with recognisable common values; to strive and survive as best one could with limited resources and, when possible, to enjoy one's life to the full in a healthy and creative way.

Whether it was the natural spores of the trees and grasses dissolved in the cool night air, or a slight excess of oxygen when compared to the phlogiston of the dirty town; or perhaps even the slight elevation of the local topography? … but it is unarguable fact that one slumbered deeply and contentedly through the night in this haven of havens!

Another morning. There are stone walls and heavy beams straddling the walls. Windows and doors are the vacant eyes of a building under construction. The newcomer has decided to raise the ridge plank first before hoisting the rafters one at a time. He has a tower structure of crude timbers, blocks and steel rope. Using his car he will pull the rope to hoist the ridge beam. Pausing for a rest and a drink of water the newcomer took in the panorama of hills and forest about him. Only nature filled his view with no sign of a habitation anywhere on the landscape before him. A gentle breeze wafted and blew the high branches of river gums back and forth in a gentle rhythm. The sun reflected from thousands of individual leaves in a sparkly display like Christmas tinsel, delighting the heart and soul of the builder. He paused to reflect about his plans and life in this haven of stream, hill and tree far from the bustle of his own childhood. He dwelt on his beautiful wife with her fair skin, blue eyes and long dark hair. He gazed down on his two small sons with their rosy cheeks and golden hair, playing in the sand pile. Pausing for those few moments he experienced the ultimate sensation of joy and happiness with his life, his luck and fortune, in his creation and that of his maker. It passed entirely through his being as a wave bringing a tremor to both his body and soul.

Sally Blanchard

Over: Stone walls and skeletal roof frame

Goldmine

The boy stood before the gaping mouth of the mine entrance to the King Castle gold mine. Apart from old John Bird that pulled out a bit of rock during the summer months, the mine had not heard the sound of stampers and crushers seriously at work since 1912. Outside the day was warm. He looked down the valley at the tree clad blue-grey hills and watched shadows of small clouds slip-slide over the forest and gullies giving them a momentary dark olive appearance. He could not see the water but the tops of river gums traced the path of the meandering creek. Their leaves shimmered, reflecting millions of small flashes of sunlight as they played and danced in the random puffs of zephyrs hardly breathed. A pair of wedge-tailed eagles soared and circled high overhead. The newcomer was hammering and the blows reverberated down the valley. Despite the presence, the boy was happy. Perhaps at last this stranger had become part of his favourite haunt, no less familiar than rock, tree, bird and pouched herbivore. With his torch switched on he ventured in.

After eighty metres the tunnel turned a sharp left. It was narrow and low with just a few centimetre of space above his head when standing erect. Before venturing further he looked back to see clearly the blue of day as a small distant rectangle. Following the new direction he found timber work in many places holding up an unstable roof of broken rock. Gingerly, he passed under these fearful shored up bridges not daring to lean on an upright or issue a murmur from his lips. Eventually he arrived at the foot of a long ladder leading up and away into darkness. The boy had never before climbed the ladder or progressed further along this tunnel.

"Now don't you be going anywhere near them old gold mines" his mother had warned before he had left home. The boy wore no helmet when he commenced to ascend the ladder. His torch was strapped to his wrist in case it slipped from his grip. A little way up he noticed the rock was black, smooth and shiny. He chipped at it with a small prospector's hammer stuffing pieces of the hard black quartz inside his jeans' pocket. Eventually, squeezing past a large rock wedged between ladder and the shaft wall, he attained the next level. A large cleft bore to his left side where the gold bearing ore had been cleared away. Several horizontal poles wedged in maybe almost a hundred years before were the only protection from a sliding wall of rock. All was quiet and eerie. No miners hammer had struck here in earnest in the passing of that century. Moving along a narrow ledge to the right his foot struck against iron drilling rods scattered on the floor. These drill bits had been driven by strong and hardy men in the 1880's and 90's to remove the ore body. The miners had followed the seam horizontally and vertically until it had been exhausted. Further to the right the boy reached a large cavern where particularly rich ore had been removed more recently. On shining his torch around the boy discovered some good pieces of ore showing positive signs of gold. "Hmm" he thought "this looks like recent work and at right angles to the original vein." Though young, he was astute in these things, learning a cunning ability of judgement and appraisal from the many surface expeditions with his father. He sat for a while and remembered the voice and words of is dad: "… and there was old John Bird used to come to these parts and camp to eek out a little ore. Even built a mini treatment plant to squeeze out the gold. Some say he made a tidy sum o' it in the 1950's working on his own".

The boy cracked a large piece of rock and placed a few shards in his pockets. At that moment his torched went out. He struck at it several times with the palm of his hand but to no avail. It wasn't merely dark; it was black as if he were totally blind. The air was not at all cold. Fear crept deeply into the boy's heart and mind and he shook a little. He wanted to cry out but he knew it was of no use. He remembered he had a box with perhaps six or so matches left in his pocket. If he could make it to the lower level he could crawl along the passage 'til he turned the corner. The difficulty was getting back along the narrow ledge to the ladder; it was perhaps only twenty or thirty metres away. If he were careful with the matches, he could reach the ladder. The rest should be easy even though scary. The thought struck him that nobody knew he was here!

He lit his first match and was able to scramble to the ledge. He had eight matches in all but they were difficult to light as the box was old and crumpled. Successively he lit his matches until he saw the ladder within grasp after which he was unable to light another. He sat for a few moments, frightened even by the sound of his own breathing. Briefly, he felt a slight tremor in the ground like the rumbling of a giant's stomach. He manoeuvred himself to straddle the ladder and slowly descended, his heart pounding. The final step soon arrived. He gingerly crawled along the passage of the lower level feeling his way as if by the antennae of a giant insect. After what seemed like an eternity, he reached the corner to see the rectangle of light. It was no longer blue and bright but a dull grey. He lifted himself to his feet and walked the distance to the entrance. He was free and safe again.

It was cloudy now and a pitter patter of fine rain cooled his face. Slowly he composed himself and felt an inner glow knowing he had survived his ordeal. He had no immediate plan to return to the entrails of this mine alone. A flock of pied currawongs cawed and scampered about the slope as he moved gently down through juvenile box trees to the creek. There he dipped his hands into a clear pool and washed them and then his face. His clothes and jacket were covered in yellow dust. He was sure to get a smack around the ear from his mum on arriving home. But in his pockets he held his treasure of black quartz and striated dense yellow shards of ore. He would set these in pride of place in his

MacIntyre Kitchen

bedroom. His cover story, though not believed, was that he got into a scrap at the footy ground. Despite his mother's careworn countenance and gruff way, she loved the boy dearly and felt for his solitude and self-imposed lonely ways.

After an hour of punishment in his room his mum called out:

"Snaggs an' chips fer your dinner son, better clean yerself up an' get to the kitchen. Then we will watch a bit of telly. There may even be a bit o' liquorice to chew on later!"

His dad was sitting reading the racing page of the Herald and sipping at a bottle of Fosters Lager. He would probably get through six of these ere the night was done and he'd haul himself into bed- after all, it was Saturday. Or maybe he'd slip down to Frenchy's for a game of cards. He would take ten dollars and no more. Sometimes he came home with nought, sometimes with a small win. At least he had the sense not to play big. Yes, he'd done time and made some mistakes in his life but he cared for his family and did the best he could when one considers the limitations of his education. He had left school at fourteen and took on mainly labouring jobs. A bit of petty thieving at fifteen landed him as a guest of His Majesty, but on meeting Mary at the age of twenty, Daniel MacIntyre had matured and settled down with purpose. Since his accident he was even a little more considerate to his wife and kids. "We'll do it here for a spell, maybe another two years at most then head down to the west of Tassie love" he would often say to his wife. "Near the beach… it will be a better life for all of us! Plenty of timber mills down there lookin' fer blokes wi' experience"

And that was his plan. At thirty six you'd have placed him at ten or fifteen years older. That is the life of the working man, even in our modern time.

The MacIntyres had a historical connection with Eastern Victoria as well as Tasmania. The first MacIntyre arrived at Port Jackson from

Scotland in 1821 as a paying passenger but shared with female convicts. After a brief try at sheep farming Dan's ancestors sailed to Port Phillip and then on to the goldfields of Ballarat. Later some went to live in Hobart after working as bakers on the goldfields of Eastern Victoria around Battery. Here was Dan again in Eastern Victoria but now with a hankering to return to Tasmania.

"Yes, maybe after the insurance pay-out" he continued, "then we can make a clean break and a new start!"

School

Snowy Ballscratcher earned his crude nickname for his teaching style and methodology. Whilst the students read the assigned text he would be at the front of the class with a paperback of dubious quality in one hand and the other constantly fiddling deep inside his trouser pocket. Perhaps he had no pocket lining or perhaps he was merely jingling coins. However the boys in the class had their own theory. Invariably he would fall asleep with the uncanny ability to continue to fiddle like the cod-fisherman in church in that famous of books "Sailing Alone Around the World" by Joshua Slocum. The man had been a Chaplain stationed with an Australian regiment in Singapore when the Japs arrived on their bicycles. He had survived an unpleasant three and a bit years in the notorious Changi prisoner of war camp, Singapore. His short cropped hair was neat with a few curls hanging at the front. It was snow white. As a returned serviceman he was given a teaching position as English master. He continued also as an Anglican Chaplain. The congregation in the small wooden church was pitifully small comprising mostly five or six of the elderly representatives of the community. Strangely this could swell to hundreds for a funeral. Anglicans made up the greater proportion of the area but did not attend church. Snowy was near retirement when the boy attended the secondary school.

Harry Wallbanger was a disturbed young man of Scottish heritage, tall with golden wavy hair and thick square glasses. He reminded one of a young Clark Kent- reporter from the Daily Planet, although Harry hated confrontation and was in no way a superman! He also tried in vain to teach the 'tongue of our forefathers'. One morning in extreme angst he punched a hole in the blackboard and hence earned his name.

The newcomer tried to teach Science but failed miserably during his early years due to exuberance in diagrams, language and philosophical inclinations that the poor students found almost impossible to follow. Some of the senior girls liked his appearance so much that they wanted to bed him, sometimes rubbing their immature breasts against him as they passed him in the doorway to class. The newcomer had an everlasting problem with young single female teachers and particularly student teachers that would be at the school for a month or so. They would not desist from sitting on his knee in the staff room in full view of other staff. Even in this remote community the newcomer had problems with women. Some envied him but the newcomer had a darling wife and two beautiful young children to care for. He had all that any man could wish for and did not wish to jeopardise his life's ambitions and love of family. After all, was he not a Christian man?

Mr Tiger was the senior teacher and a portly man of whom the community thought the world. He was a go-getter and a doer and built his whole life around school, athletics, swimming, junior football and Scouting. He was almost saintly in his demeanour and presided on every committee that existed. Unfortunately, Tiger's one weakness (and by no means a mere foible) was his proclivity and uncontrollable desire to fondle young boys. In brief, he was a nonce! His photographic collection of 'boys' was prolific. He got away with his disturbed inclinations for years until caught red-handed with naughty photos of his own students some years later. He was acting Principal at the time. After the court proceedings and media hullabaloo there were still many members of the community that just did not believe his guilt! Naturally he did incalculable damage to the Scouting movement. But his case was not rare! Each year within the state of Victoria alone, at least half a dozen teachers from primary or secondary schools are dismissed for some sexual misdemeanour involving their charges!

Then there was the Driver husband and wife team. Maggie Driver was English teacher cum librarian of noble aspiration and an old

Presbyterian College girl from the upper end of the class spectrum. Husband Dave was a radical History teacher also with long black Jesus hair and beard, fashionable in the 70's and 80's. Dave was an inspiration to the school and taught history perhaps unconventionally but in a manner that was much appreciated by his students. He loved to take them on expeditions to local historical spots, mines, geological places of interest, aboriginal encampments and similar. He would make use of drama and film in his teaching which the students were most enthusiastic about. He was an avid writer of history particularly relating to Aboriginals and workers unions associated with the coal industry. They were concurrently constructing their house from mud brick at Islay.

Jerry Longshank was a science teacher, a sheep farmer and a gentleman. He had served as a navigator with the RAAF during WWII. He was a good story teller and would enthral us with his tales of navigating aboard the famous Lancaster bombers stationed in England in the 1940's. It was Jerry that sold a small wild piece of land to the newcomer. Jerry had a son and two daughters. Sadly, his son was killed in an accident in America.

'Turn to Page Thirty Three' was a puritanical recalcitrant mathematics cum art teacher, wanting in teaching talent other than "turn to page 33 and complete all the exercises". He was the predictable product of a boy growing up with elder sisters and strict church school indoctrination. He turned out a bitter person with little Christian charity and a large dosage of the super-critic! At this time, he too was building his own dwelling on a remote heavily timbered bush-block. Hopefully the toll of years and life's experience has mellowed him a tad?

Quantum Hogg was a short, dynamic and humorous art-craft teacher and perhaps one of the most intelligent of persons one could meet. His wit was so sharp that it sailed right over all most of the time, to the annoyance of some. He was also an owner builder preferring mud brick as the medium for his dwelling. He was a no-nonsense man and the students liked him very much.

Amazing Gerty O'Malley was a little neurotic but an excellent and dedicated English teacher married to a beef and sheep farmer at Islay. They were a very kind hearted family of six and much loved in the district. Gerty was most kind to the newcomer and his wife, often providing gifts for their children.

A short Austrian named Helmut took German classes and lived and worked his five acre block at the foot of the Nunniong mountains. He was married to a charming lady of mixed English-Maori blood. Helmut was extremely proud of his mini-farm and supplied the staff each morning with milk from his Jersey cow. His only shortcoming (apart from his height) was that he thought Adolf was basically a good bloke and carefully had his birthday etched onto his classroom calendar!

The laboratory technician was the youngest son of a family of a half dozen siblings. Glazed Dave or Smokey Dave was a true believer in socialism and a dedicated 'back to the earth' character. He was also building a bush paradise at some distance from the main road where he and his charming little family kept chooks, ducks and bees. They worked extremely hard in their orchard and vegetable garden and came as near to self-sufficiency as is humanly possible. Dave was a keen member of the film society and became close friends with the newcomer.

The home economics teacher was a dish with long golden locks and the daughter of a local sheep farmer of Orkney Isles ancestry. The newcomer, to tell the truth, was more than a little infatuated but remained disciplined!

"I'm thinking about you all the night and the day-
Got this feeling about you that just won't go away
To kiss your mouth is all I want to say
Because I .... "

There were also the drifters, mainly fresh graduates that came for a year at most then moved on. The Principal was from 'across the road' at the Primary School and had jurisdiction over both schools. He was a balding man, lean and single that was of a vague disposition. Perhaps he was shell-shocked during the war. He had no grip on the affairs of either school and kept no accounts. In fact, it was recorded that at a June end-of-financial-year School Council Meeting he stood up and said "the school budget and accounts for the year are too complex and numerous to be determined!" And that was his financial report!

The boy had passed through primary school with modest success and had been at the secondary school for three years now. He had few friends (although some of the girls found his comical antics amusing and befriended him). However some of the teachers would openly comment that the father was a criminal and that the boy would never amount to much. The Tiger was fairly instrumental in seeing the boy leave school early, not quite before his fifteenth birthday. There remained an 8 mm film at the school library's archives from one of Dave's history classes where the boy, wearing his blue raincoat, brassard depicting Thor's hammer and with some carbon smeared above his lip and grease on his hair, performed a rather convincing parody of Adolf Hitler, clicking heels and giving the Nazi salute. Dave admitted it was one of the funniest things he had ever recorded as a teacher of drama in history. Did this episode, however, seal the fate of the boy in this remote community? It is a theory of nefarious aspect!

The Tiger somehow brought more pressure to bear and by manipulation at School Council forced the boy out of school before the end of his third form with no final report. Most of the teachers were unaware of the true nature of these underhand and disgraceful proceedings and were given a pre-Christmas minute that the boy's parents had withdrawn him from the school… later to be determined clearly as a cruel and blatant lie!

The boy lingered at home for several months, visiting all his favourite haunts as he was apt to do before being employed in his father's footsteps at the timber mill. He was just fifteen years.

The work was repetitive but not too exhausting. However the hours were long, usually from 5.30 am 'til 5 pm. The money wasn't much but he gave most of it to his mum who was most appreciative. The little extra made her life easier and she was able to provide better food and clothes for the family.

More than a year had passed since the accident when one morning Dan was called to the office.

"Daniel" said the manager formally, "you know we applied for your insurance claim after the accident, well its here in this morning's mail. You have been awarded fourteen thousand dollars on a take it or leave it basis. You could go to court on this but it could take years. What do you say?"

Dan was not a union man. He had no conception of what an arm was worth. His pay was certainly far reduced now that he had simpler tasks to perform. To him this amount was a fortune. He thought of his plan of escape with his family down to Tasmania and a new life. The shrewd manager pushed forward a piece of paper.

"If you accept this amount now, all you have to do is sign at the bottom here and I will present you immediately with the cheque from the insurance company. What do you think?"

Of course the company preferred the smallish pay-out as it would keep their future insurance premium down. Claims in the hundreds of thousands would certainly swiftly result in a hike of the company's annual insurance coverage payment. Had the manager been a decent bloke he would have advised that Dan speak with the Timber Mill Union Representative first and think about it for a few days. But that wasn't the way of it. Dan was a basic salt of the earth man and quietly acquiesced.

"She'll be right Mr Vizard. Where do I sign?"

And so the deal was done.

As far as Dan was concerned, he was happy to be on his way to Tasmania.

Mitch said "You're a bloody fool Dan, you should've netted at least a couple of hundred grand!"

"Yeah" piped in the Russian "they're just takin' advantage of you Dan, those money-grubbing back-stabbing bastards!"

Dan took the money and promptly submitted a month's resignation.

"But dad, I don't want to leave here. I have a job now and I have my exploring and fishing" implored the boy to his father.

"Things will be better in Tassie son, believe me. You will have the beach as well as the forest to roam in."

In the final agreement, the boy stayed at the mill-house of an adjacent family. Not being dissuaded, he continued to work at the mill.

"OK, you and mum, the kid 'n' sis go on ahead. I'll see my term out and join you at Christmas!"

The boy was adamant in staying at least to the end of the year. He could save a little and pay his own way down to Tasmania.

The day the MacIntyres left, Mrs Mack wept openly and hugged her son. "You be a good boy and write regularly you promise?"

"Yes mum, don't worry. The time 'll pass soon enough and we will have Christmas together in the new place."

For a lad of fifteen years he seemed so grown up and certain of himself. His father shook his hand and was proud. His mother cried all the way down to Maintown in the Holden car, a little more than an hour's journey. She felt robbed of her son who was still a boy really. Dan consoled her.

"Don't worry ma, he's a strong boy. Christmas will be here in no time… no time at all!"

The car wormed and threaded its way parallel to the MacMillan River. Most of the journey was through forest before the last few kilometres into Maintown where forest at last gave way to open farmland. At the brow of the last hill the sprawling town was seen and beyond the Lakes that led to the sea. Mary would never return to Rushing Creek. Dan would make just one brief journey back and sooner than he had reckoned upon!

But the writer is getting ahead of himself with the story. Let us go back a time to before the boy had left school and all was reasonably well with his life….. He was no scholar, but made no trouble for the teachers. His interests lay in practical science, particularly anything to do with trees, animals and rocks. Although only a small part of the curriculum, his knowledge of these things pertinent to the immediate district was far above those of other students. Even his science teacher on occasion would ask him to identify a tree or name a marsupial. The boy also liked drawing, mainly with pencil or charcoal and was quite adept at portraying natural scenery. Above all, he was an energetic collector of stones, rocks, bones and fossils and had an extraordinary collection jammed into his bedroom. He was always close by to Mr Driver when on a field excursion.

But another intruder into the boy's life was close at hand; one who would at first frighten him, bewilder him and lastly kindle a deep and trusting friendship.

"Seig ….. Seig ….. Seig ….. "

Revelry

The boy, accompanied by his younger brother, baby sister, mum and dad were to be seen at the River Inn on this Saturday night. It was a small family pub tucked away off the main road at Islay (pronounced eye-lah), Islay being one of the four small villages or hamlets of the Shire with around three hundred inhabitants. This autumn night held a distinct chill in the air; but inside a wood burner along with many enlivened bodies gave the lounge room a cosy and warm atmosphere. Another small open fire burned inside the compact bar area with a solid red box log that would smoulder for hours yet, yielding a good heat to the throng. The walls were adorned mainly with football and netball icons… past victories of the blue and gold, old team portraits, sashes and other sport's paraphernalia. Farmers, timber workers, tree fellers, road gang, school teachers and various other government employees mixed together with children and dogs about their feet. The beer flowed and the voices roared in a cacophony of story telling and laughter- all in competition in a rosy and cheery melee. Red beards, grey beards, black curly beards and crimson flushed cheeks rose and fell, bobbing as a sea of talking heads in the hooley. Many had come with family to eat a steak or seafood platter at the family restaurant. The publicans were a couple: Big Ben, a burley fellow of a genteel and placid nature and his woman Lanky, a tall blond girl with a bubbly nature and always keen to please the customer. Apparently it was said that she could throw a forceful punch if circumstances necessitated. But the clientele, though raucous, did not put up with any violent behaviour inside. Would-be troublemakers, rare as they may be, were quickly bundled out the door into the cold night air.

The boy watched the pool players take their shots, careful to be at a safe distance from the table. By 9 pm the melee was at its height when the boy espied the newcomer seated at table with almost a dozen acquaintances talking, smoking, drinking and laughing. The talk was mostly of a political or philosophical nature, else about the progress of their various construction projects- their homes. These were in the main chalkies (school teachers) and owner builders. All had escaped the environs of city life to bring up their children in this pleasant nook of East Gippsland. They were idealistic, young and carefree souls but also individualistic in their approaches to building a dwelling and home among the gum trees. At once, the guitars and banjo appeared and the round table burst into song. Australian, Scottish and English folk songs; contemporary and of yore as well as a sprinkling of Irish rebel songs filtered through the smoky air of this denizen. The boy leaned against the wall of the lounge room absorbed in the character of the newcomer as he sang the ancient Scottish ballad "Wilde Mountain Thyme".

> "Oh the summer time is a-coming
> And the trees are sweetly bloomin'
> And the wild mountain thyme
> Grows around the blooming heather
> Will ye go lassie go?"

The boy was much taken by the fusion of beauty and sadness of the lyric but more emotionally struck by the richness and timbre of the voice of the newcomer. He warmed to this man with the golden mane of a lion and fierce red beard, despite the fact he had intruded into his personal bush retreat and playground that he considered his alone. The newcomer was not aware of the presence of the boy or his family in the pub that night. As the evening wore on the singers became more animated and louder. Sweat trickled down their rosy faces and more beer trickled down their parched throats to tickle and caress the vocal

Hooley at the River Inn

chords. Glazed John, huddled near his beautiful young wife Fonda, now took up his banjo and began to sing “Poor Ned”. Immediately there was violent clapping and a thumping of boots as the crowd joined in with the chorus. Towards midnight as the crowd fell away, some more serious and slow laments took over before the pub was finally cleared. Only the glow of crackling embers and smell of beer, tobacco and human sweat permeated this empty and silent hall as time moved steadily on and the hubbub away. With stringent laws for drivers such nights are seldom if ever experienced at the River Inn these days.

> “I can drink an’ no be drunk an’
> I can fight and ne’er be slain,
> I can court wi’ another man’s lass an’
> still be welcome to me ain”

A slip of cloud skimmed over the gibbous moon. The night was still and the newcomer, his wife and two small sons were bedded down for the night in their steel shed, the wood stove stacked and irradiating sufficient heat to keep them cosy. The newcomer sank into slumber happy with his life, happy with this small piece of paradise and happy with the choices he had made. He prayed as his mind faded for all he had and for protection over his family. For all his apparent external coarseness, he remained a Christian man. A fox barked at some distance and a boobook owl echoed his constant refrain over the murmur of the brook.

Soldier

Akimitsu Nakamura was only nineteen when he was sent as a foot soldier of 'His Imperial Japanese Forces' to the Pacific. He was among the first to enter New Guinea with the Japanese 18th Army, under Lieutenant General Hatazō Adachi, being captured by Australian troops in 1943. Having come from a small village in rural Japan close to the coastal town of Uchinoura on the southern island of Kyushu and destined to be a farmer like his father, he had not been indoctrinated to the extent of 'suicide with honour' in place of capture with dishonour. Hence he had found himself a captive of his enemy and sent to a prison camp in the heartland of New South Wales, Australia. It was here that he rubbed shoulders with the more fanatical soldiers of the Empire.

"We must make every attempt to escape and kill as many of the enemy as possible to serve the Emperor" was the daily tirade of the most senior Japanese commander. A small minority even chose the traditional ceremony of suicide- 'seppuku' (better known as 'hara-kiri' in English) for their shame and humiliation in order to join their ancestors in the hereafter.

And so it was that a detailed break-out was planned for August 5th 1944. On the eve of the escape Akimitsu said his prayers and kissed the photograph of his parents which he had been permitted to keep. The escape was messy with many soldiers becoming entangled in the barbed wire of the perimeter fence to be wounded or shot dead.

"Walk over me, walk over me!... 私上の歩行! 私上の歩行!" his comrade shouted. Thus Akimitsu was free along with hundreds of others. His only weapon was a makeshift knife which he had fashioned from a broken wood file stolen from the craft centre. By rubbing it day and night with a stone, he had honed it to a sharp and pointed weapon. The night air was cool. Akimitsu kept away from the towns and main roads and made his way south alone. He dared not to rest but pushed his way through light forest and open farmland for two days until he could go on no more. He lay comfortably and amazed at the starry heavens above him. Such an array of twinkling lights he had never experienced. Mostly he had travelled through farmland and was able to avail himself of fresh eggs and poultry along the way. He came very close to people on occasion but these were all farming families. He could not bring himself to attack and kill indiscriminately. What if foreign invaders were skulking about his beloved country? Would he want his mother, father and baby sister mercilessly to have their throats cut whilst they slept? Certainly not! He prayed for his own deliverance and the safety of his family back home. Was there a girl whom he favoured? Yes there was Etsu from his village. She was just fifteen years but they had become very close and had a secret pact that when he returned from the war they would marry. They would often sit beneath a large willow tree on the banks of the stream that flowed near the village chatting and dreaming of the future and their plans. He would bring oranges from the farm together with a little saké of the White Stallion label and sip it delightfully.

Most of the other soldiers had decided to go east to the sea and try to do as much damage along the way as was possible. All were recaptured. Akimitsu decided he would go south to the sea as he knew it was almost equidistant from Cowra and there would be fewer people along the way. Who knows, he might even capture a small sail boat and sail back to Japan. All knew that to go north was impossible and too far. Akimitsu might live from what he could catch in the ocean.

The smells of farms, animals and growing things were all familiar to him with the exception of the eucalyptus. He soon came to love its soothing effect on his tired lungs as he pushed ever south. Soon he saw great hills rising before him and he slowly ascended through the blue haze to reach almost two thousand metres above the plains behind. There were no farms here and he became cold and hungry. Patches of snow lay on the grassy meadows and under the twisted snow gums.

To get close to a kangaroo or wallaby was too difficult. They would be away over the ground far too quickly for him to catch. Along a small stream he perceived a small group of emu lazing in the flickering light from the waving branches overhead. Taking a rock he was able to crush the head by a lucky throw before they realised that danger approached. With his hands and knife he prepared the bird and roasted pieces of meat on a green stick over a small fire. He thought it tasted a little fishy but generally pleasing.

He was able to tie some stones together with a leather lace. Whenever a flock of parrots, rosellas or white cockatoos came near he would twirl his stones and bring down the occasional bird. He pressed on, eventually crossing the Great Divide and entering the hinterland of East Gippsland.

At last he descended into a narrow valley that had sheep grazing in paddocks cut squarely from the surrounding bush. He saw just two houses of timber painted white under corrugated iron roofs. Further down the valley two creeks joined and just beyond this lay the remains of a mining operation. Machines and brickwork were scattered over the dry ground where young grey box were reclaiming the once cleared area. A small log hut was empty but had the signs of occasional use. Here he found sugar and a tin of tea. He decided to risk staying in the hut overnight. He rejoiced in the simple comfort of a makeshift bed and a large mug of very sweet tea. It was not a flavour he was inclined to favour but had become accustomed at the prison camp. He awoke early to see a leveret and many rabbits scurrying around on a small field of just two acres adjacent to the hut. There was no crop, the field appearing to have lain fallow for many years. Horehound, parsley, mint and a host of other herbs grew close to the hut. Spring had arrived and to his surprise the large purple buds of a sizeable magnolia tree were opening to reveal their inner snowy petals. Nearby a blossoming cherry akin to those of his own village was scenting heavy with a constant buzz of worker bees aboard each flower collecting the nectar. It warmed his heart and brought a tear to his eye to make a small but significant nexus between here and his home so far away. It did not occur to him that these blessings were a rarity among the forests of Gippsland!

Strolling down a gentle slope for about twenty paces, he discovered a singing stream under the shade of willows. He scooped up the water. Apart from the birds and natural sounds, there was no intrusion of man. Bellbirds played sweet melodies and swallows darted through the air above him. These also he was familiar with in his native Japan as they were a seasonal migrant. Who knows, perhaps these swallows might even be from his very own village? He spent many days exploring about the old mine site. Along the creek in a cliff face of yellow mud and sand there was a tunnel. Some miner had followed a thin quartz layer of grit and pebble directly into the cliff. Inside he could tell that only a sleepy wombat was now the sole inhabitant. As the hut was used intermittently, Akimitsu decided to enter the tunnel and at the end create a small room for himself where he could rest coolly and hide away from the world. To his surprise, the old mine site contained many useful items including candles, matches and even corn stored in ten gallon steel drums. Whoever frequented this place kept a stock of materials, food and tools, much of which seemed to be from army supplies. There were even two beehives in the small field that had been so neglected, but each still contained an active colony. Akimitsu had learned from his father how to take off the honey from frames using hot water and a good sharp knife.

Rather than proceeding on to the coast he now seriously thought about staying in this small paradise for a while. After all, he reasoned, who knows, perhaps in a year or so the war will be over and he no longer need fear of being recaptured. And so it came to pass that he abandoned his mission of escape to Japan and instead gouged out his secret home in the wombat tunnel to eke out a living in this remote haven.

A miner would arrive and stay at the hut for as long as three or four weeks at a time, then not return for many more months. He usually came alone but, on occasion, accompanied with a boy Akimitsu guessed was the miner's son. One day whilst scrabbling about in an old shed adjacent to the hut he found an old valve radio. Having no battery he scoured the mine site until he located an old army truck with a battery still in place. The battery needed topping up with water and the terminals cleaned and scraped. To his utmost delight a faint crackle and sound of music emanated from the radio. There were commentaries and news in English but Akimitsu's knowledge of English was almost zero. The miner had a largish diesel generator from which he could recharge the battery from time to time. But he had to be careful. Sometimes a farmer would suddenly appear on his steed moving sheep from out of the forest. An occasional vehicle would trundle along the dirt road some one hundred metres away across the creek. But the valley was well forested here with tall river gums, blue gum and dense stands of wattle and blackwood. The chance of being seen from the road was highly unlikely.

Thus with hare, rabbits, sheep, birds and the occasional reptile for his plate, Akimitsu started to fall into a habitual pattern of life. The miner never missed the small amount of grain, sugar or tea that was carefully taken from the hut. The creek always yielded eels which were a delicacy. The years rolled by with little change and Akimitsu had grown accustomed to his solitary life.

Then he noticed that all of a sudden there was more frequent traffic on the road. In fact he counted at least two cars daily on average. This brought him some angst. Occasionally at the weekend, tourists from a local village would come for a Sunday picnic and once, even a group of school children. He looked at the male teacher with scrutiny and surprise. He was not Japanese but had a long mane of black hair and a longish black beard. Was this a Samurai or holy man he thought? Had his people conquered the land after all? But there was no other evidence.

Perhaps almost three decades had passed. Akimitsu was always cautious. He hunted early in the morning, checking his rabbit snares. He stored potatoes and dried meat for the cold of winter and avoided those times when the ghost people were around. He made wine and various elixirs from the nettles, rosehips and blackberries garnered from woods and field close by; tea from mint, clover flower or dandelion.

To his horror there now came frequent banging from the river flat just five hundred metres downstream from his secure abode. Much of the tea-tree scrub had been cleared and close under the hill a large steel shed was being erected. More miners he thought? A small red German car was often seen. A man had used a shovel, pick and axe to clear a passage from the road. This was serious. What were his intentions? Then one day he heard the peel of children's laughter and the tender voice of a woman calling. He sat and cried as he thought of Etsu and his family not seen for so many years. A schoolteacher was the only other women he had glimpsed since his self-imposed exile.

It was obvious that this family were asleep that night in the metal shed they had erected. Without thinking he approached the shed just before dawn and banged on its sides furiously with a heavy stick before retreating again into the shadows of the forest to see what would happen. A hairy young man appeared at the door in underpants and nought else. He yelled out into the silence of the cool predawn air "We're here to stay so you can jest frick off- de you hear?"

Akimitsu had picked up enough English from his radio and the miner's newspapers to get the gist of the message and like a shadow slipped back to his home in the cliff face. He pondered long on this new intrusion and wondered if he should either give himself up at last or kill the family in the dead of night. But the man and his wife's children could be no more than three or four years of age. He put this crazy thought out of his mind!

One day he was in a bit of a dream as he emerged from the tunnel to the stream just a little after dawn. There in front of him stood a boy wearing a blue coat. There was a light drizzle falling. The two simultaneously froze and merely eyed each other for many minutes. This was Akimitsu's first contact with another human in almost thirty years!

Blue wren

Akimutsu presents his sword!

Trust

Akimitsu knelt down on the wet grass. A frond of a small tree fern caressed his shoulder as he held out his hands imploringly, his eyes averted downwards. The boy stood motionless for a while uncertain of what to do and then stepping forward touched the man's clasped hands.

"Who are you mister; what are you doing here?" said the boy haltingly; and then… "is there anything I can do for you; are you in pain?"

The man started to rock a little back and forth letting out a quiet but incomprehensible sound, almost like the whine from an injured animal. Suddenly he composed himself and stood upright and stiff in his soldier's posture.

"I Akimitsu Nakamura of His Majesty's Impelial Army. I sulender sword to you!"

Seeing he had no sword in his hand, the man quickly looked about and picking up a dead branch from the ground, presented it to the boy giving a deep bow. The boy could not contain himself further. Fear had dissipated at once and he gave out a light hearted titter.

"Oh thank you mister. It is most generous of you to surrender your sword. I see you like to play at drama as so do I. But tell me, where have you come from and why are you here in my forest?"

The boy had been past the tunnel many times and though not easily seen due to shrubbery at the mouth, he knew of its existence. Knowing that a wombat lived there he had never given it a thought to explore further.

"This your folest? Oh please no harm me; I just poor soldier living in hole in glound waiting for war to end."

The drizzle had stopped and shafts of bright sunlight fell to the spot where the two stood. The boy sat down on the grassy bank and began breaking twigs and throwing them into a pool before them.

"And what war do you speak of?" said the boy. "Are you Vietnamese?"

The man did not comprehend this.
"The war between Amelica and Japan. Is still going or stop now?"
"Are you serious? That war ended long before I was born. Germany and Japan surrendered in 1945 I think it was. Are you kidding me still? Are we playing some sort of game?"
Akimitsu sat down hesitantly on the bank next to the boy. His movements were slow and his mind lost in some distant world. He began a chant in low tremulous tones, a song from his village that he learned as a child whilst still in a dreamy state. Suddenly he broke off.
"It is eleventh month 1972 yes?" he enquired of the boy.
"Yes, it is the 24th of November- nearly Christmas" said the boy animatedly. "What do you do for Christmas? Do you visit someone or do they visit you?"
The man thought of the miner. He usually showed up in mid December.
"Oh yes, someone usually come Clistmas" he replied absently.
"Then you live somewhere close?" ventured the boy.
"Why I live in this vely cave" said the man pointing across the creek with a twig. "You want see my house?"
The boy felt a little uneasy at this suggestion and began to rise.
"Maybe another time. I ought to be getting along now."
"I not hurt you. Lemember, I give sword to you as honolable person and soldier. It glate honour to me. Come, I make a nice tea yes?"
The boy was still hesitant but a feeling of empathy swept over his body and he could see that it meant a lot to the man in his ragged clothes. He was not at all tall, being wiry, thin and a little bent over in posture.
"OK, proceed then" said the boy in the blue raincoat, pointing a stick towards the hole.
The tunnel was low and they crept along on hands and feet. There was wombat dung on the floor. They reached a T-junction and crept to the right. A piece of hessian hung down. Pushing past this they were

suddenly in a small room with a single candle burning. There was a strong odour of beeswax and the soldier quickly lit several more large candles.

There was not a lot to be seen in this small room. A shelf contained a wooden statue with a candle at either side of a faded photograph. A kangaroo skin lay on the floor.

"This where I play (pray). That my family. It first chamber I make. Come, come!"

With head bowed forward he led the way down another short tunnel in which one could barely stand. Through a wooden door with sneck and latch this time, low and behold, they were in a much larger room with low ceiling. It had been very carefully constructed with upright poles and a ceiling of thin box logs. The floor was entirely of small wooden blocks fitted very carefully together. Again the smell of beeswax pervaded the inside. With many large candles lit, the soldier beckoned the boy to sit on a small wooden chair by a table. All were meticulously carved from the native box and blackwood that grew prodigiously around in the forest outside. There were bowls and other adornments plus utensils of metal that had been scrounged from the mine site and fashioned into useful things. In a side alcove the soldier heated some water over a fire and made some tea for the boy. He was still in a state of amazement. Slowly quaffing at the piquant liquor heavily laced with honey, he queried:

"You did all this Mister? You have really lived here since the war?"

"Well, I suppose and I suppose I did."

The soldier began to look about his own place as if seeing it himself for the first time and gave out a little chuckle and nodded his head satisfactorily. The man had a longish wispy beard and wore blue baggy trousers and long-sleeved shirt with broad cuffs fashioned from the same material. His face was drawn and deeply furrowed but his dark

eyes seemed to twinkle like those of an ancient sage. The boy thought the man to be seventy or there about.
"How old are you now Mister?" enquired the boy.
"Well… must think." He approached a square board hanging on the wall with many small pegs and holes.
"I must fifty two years now. And you?"
"Oh I am almost fifteen Sir… and where did you say you were from?"
"Family oligin (origin) from Hokkaido Island in north Japan but honolable glandfather move to Kyushu in south. Now glow many olange and vegetable."
The boy sipped his tea listening intently.
"Now tell young man. You see ladio (radio) there. It not work since twelve years. Need new glass in it. Maybe you get fix for me. Now what news of world? Tell me about Japan. Do you know Japan?"
"I know everyone drives Japanese cars now Sir. And Australia sends a lot of iron ore there. We learned that from the geography teacher Mr Driver. I know the Americans dropped a big bomb on Hiroshima in 1945 which ended the war. That's about all I really knows Sir."
The soldier sat stroking his beard and thought for a long time.
"Dlink tea my boy. Now please me… you not tell anyone about me just yet. Can you keep seclet?" he said with a melancholy and pleading expression. "I need think and decide what do, you understand?"
"I think so Mister. It must come of a shock to you to find out these things. But don't worry Mister, I's good at secrets… and I will try and get the radio fixed for you if you like? Is there anything else you would like me to fetch?"
"Just ladio for now. But you must plomise keep me seclet. No tell anyone I here OK?"
Carefully the soldier wrapped the old General Electric in newspaper and tied the parcel with some twine. Carefully the boy receded down

the way he had come and finally, again out into the fresh morning with all its sweet sounds and smells.

Old man Harris the school cleaner was a bit of a radio buff. He also owned a small second-hand shop in the village.

“Be hard to get the valve replacements” he said on looking over the unit. “I think old Cherry down at MacMillan’s Crossing might have some bits an’ pieces. I know he was in the British RAF as a radio technician during the war.”

Sure enough old Cherry’s eyes lit up on seeing the old radio.

“Yeah, haven’t seen this p’rticular model afore but I has some equivalents for the tubes. Just leave it with me for a couple of days.”

On returning a few days later old Cherry was beaming with pride as he demonstrated the radio working again.

“It’s a beauty, where did you find the piece?”

“Oh, out at the old King Castle goldmine” replied the boy sheepishly.

“I’m not surprised at that. Old John Bird has a lot of antiquated gear there dating back to the First World War and a lot of Yank stuff too, including trucks. Well this little chap should go for a bit longer. Has long wave, medium, short and short short. Could almost listen to astronauts on the moon” was his final judgement. He flipped switches and twirled knobs until he picked up the ABC coming in faintly from Traralgon.

“Night time would be interestin’” he added “should be able to pick up Radio America, hams an’ all sorts from around the world. Jest needs a long stretch of copper wire strung up in the trees!”

“Thank you so much Mr Cherry” said the boy “how much do I owe you?”

“Just a couple of dollars for the valves. The work was pure pleasure.”

The boy took the radio home and set it up in his bedroom not knowing when he would get the opportunity to return to the King Castle mine. He lay in his bed that night twiddling knobs on the 1930's GE radio, picking up everything from satellites to cosmic music.

"Switch that bloody noise off" bellowed his father around midnight. Soon the boy slumbered, his mind swirling with all that had occurred these last couple of weeks. Was there really a Japanese soldier hiding in a wombat hole near the mine or had his mind engineered such a fantastic story? In the morning he awoke and looked at the chocolate Bakelite facade of the old radio.

"I guess it must all be true" he muttered to himself as he arose to face the new day.

The boy had two intrusions to his world now... the newcomer and the soldier. The soldier also had two intrusions to his world... the newcomer and now the boy. The newcomer celebrated his new world and did not intend any intrusions. His new world was built for himself by himself yes- but moreover, for his loving wife and dear children whom he loved more than anything. He would strive, he would build his nest and he would protect. That was his nature and value.

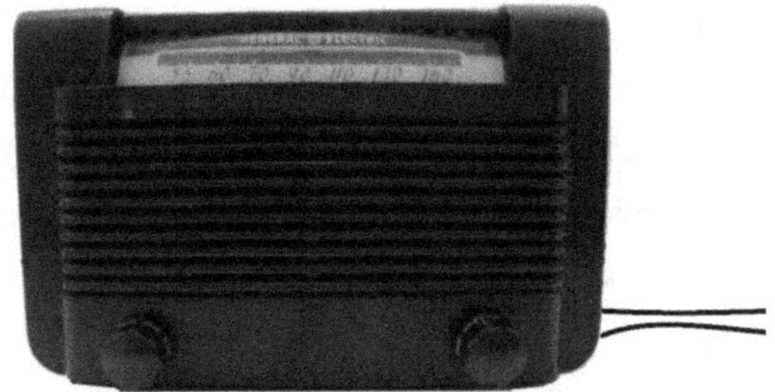

Old 1930s General Electric radio

Shearing

The newcomer visited those teachers living on a remote farm at Islay, Dave and Maggie Driver. More appropriately we should call Dave 'the historian' as that is what he is widely known as. However, a tag does little to describe a man and other tags such as 'the poet' or 'the writer' or 'the prospector' or 'the man of the mountain' might easily supplant. However we shall remain with the historian! They lived in a rented farm house that stood on a small knoll. It had a tight wired fence around the house to keep stock out and away from the fruit trees and vegetable garden surrounding. A river flowed about eighty metres from the house which needed to be forded on any visitation. The newcomer and his family spent many a fine evening with the Drivers. They were very close and had shared experiences in camping, caving and climbing adventures at an earlier time with their university club. The newcomer and the historian loved to sing folk ballads, share their knowledge of new songs and lyrics and could pass hours contenting themselves in this manner, supplemented by bottles of beer. The house was about a hundred years old and belonged to the O'Malleys, a sheep farming family of Irish stock with a moderate farm of some 800 acres and several hundred sheep and cattle herd. O'Malley liked a singsong and would invite his teacher friends for a barbeque to his own home on the other side of the river. The grandparents also lived close at hand.

O'Malley would love to finish the evening with port and Villiger cigars which he generously shared with his friends. His wife Girty had borne him three strapping lads and a strapping daughter. As aforementioned, she was also a teacher at the school.

"Te get through the hard times wi' farming' tis better yer marry a Govenmint worker" was O'Malley's father's advice. And so he married Girty. But that wasn't his intended reason; one could see at a glance that he loved Girty very much!

Between the two houses stood an ancient shearing shed that was built in the early days of settlement (circa 1850) when the whole of Islay was one station of a hundred thousand acres and more. Although now ironed over, there still remains to this day remnants of a shingle and bark roof underneath. The shearing shed is well known to artists both local and from afar, being sketched and painted a thousand times over. Now the newcomer had never witnessed a shed in action before during shearing and so he cajoled O'Malley until he relinquished and allowed him to work a weekend in the new shed.

The sky was clear and blue and the morning crisp and hoary when the newcomer showed for the day. There were three shearers, one a local old hand and two itinerants- one a Kiwi (New Zealander) and another down from New South Wales. O'Malley was there to oversee the work accompanied by the table workers, the press operator and the wool classer. The shearers used mechanical shears driven by a rotating shaft above them connected by gearing to an electric motor. No clicking of hand-shears here! Each shearer would drag his jumbuck from the pen and shear the wool away in one continuous piece. The tar-boy would apply an antiseptic mix to any deep cuts. The table hands would pick up the whole fleece and fling it dexterously onto the table. Here the dags and soiled fringes (skirtings) were pulled away so that the fleece was reasonably clean. The grader (or more accurately, wool classer) would decide on the fineness of the wool and it would then be thrown into an appropriate bin waiting to be pressed into a bale. The work was hard and went on continuously but with banter and laughter along the way. The young Kiwi was certainly the 'gun' shearer notching up 40 sheep by lunchtime, two or three ahead of the other two. When a bin was half full, the wool would be placed into a hessian bag hanging limply in the

Over: O'Malley shearing shed

cage of the baling machine or wool press. Every so often it was switched on and a steel plate would descend to compress the wool. A set of steel skewers would be driven in to hold the pack in place whilst the next few fleeces were added and so on until the bale was tight and full. The top would be stitched and metal stencils placed over the bail and painted over to impress the code of the farm, the grade of the wool and the weight. 'Fine Merino' was in great demand at this time, being shipped off to England, Italy and Asia to be milled into cloth for suits, skirts and the like. It was always coined in the first half of the 20th century that Australia's economy rode on the sheep's back... and true it was!

The odours of sweat and wool grease permeated the air. In the shadows stood the boy. His humble job was to sweep up the dags and skirtings from the floor and throw them into a special bin. He said little but watched the men at work with a keen eye. The newcomer assisted with the baling machine. It was difficult to decide how much pressure was adequate to compress a bale. Inserting the skewers was exceedingly difficult requiring more skill than muscle but impossible without muscle! Smoko at mid-morn went on for just twenty minutes where all would rest and consume very large tin mugs of sweet tea. The Kiwi brought his own flask of 'magic tea' whose ingredients were a guarded secret. At lunch the goodly Mrs O'Malley (Girty) brought over an absolute feast of braised lamb and chutney sangers (sandwiches) and a gallon more of the hot sweet tea. The newcomer enjoyed such sumptuous fare and was entertained by the commencement of serious card playing by some of the workers whilst others played a game of 'two-up'. Money changed hands but not substantial amounts, just enough for the players enjoyment without any serious damage to their pockets. The boy fell to slumber in a corner. No work was taken up again for about an hour- then it was on again! Having started at 6 am, the men worked on until four in the afternoon. It was extremely hot and uncomfortable in the shed during the latter hours with the sweat streaming from the bulging muscles of the shearers. The Kiwi finished on 85 and the others on 80 and 78 respectively. These days, with wider electric combs and cooler sheds, a good shearer can complete close to 200 sheep per day. But it is back-breaking work and not an occupation one would want to participate 'til old age. The days of shearing with hand shears were indeed the days of iron men.

> "Click go the shears boys, click click click
> Wide is his bow and his hand moves quick
> The ringer looks around and is beaten by a blow
> And curses the old swagger with the bare-bellied Jo!"

The boy slept in the car on the way home. He worked in the shed for ten days but decided he would try for a job at the Timber Mill. Shed life was not for him!

Ja'atnegarra boy shares cave with alpine dingo

Mountain

Of course there are so many mountains in the vicinity of Rushing Creek and the boy had been lucky enough to visit many in his few years due to his father's love of fishing and a natural urge to escape. Of all that were on offer though, he had two favourites: the Chinaman's hut at Nunniong and the Cobberas Number 2. These had special memories for him and in the 1960's and 70's each was not so well trodden as perhaps now.

MacIntyre had an old Holden utility of 1950's ilk that he had picked up cheap in Maintown. Before the accident he would shoot off at least once each month into the bush with the whole family or, on more vigorous trips, just his elder son.

Ah Chow had been a bit of a loner and built his log cabin on the Nunniong plateau in the nineteen thirties. It was a simple one room affair but of ample size and with a large fireplace at one end. Scant furniture and a simple bed for slumber in the rarefied air laden with the scents of eucalyptus and flowering shrubbery of the high plains. Why he preferred this solitary life was his own personal choice and cannot really be fathomed. But on staying a weekend in his hut, it was easy to appreciate the peace of the bush and the reward to soul and mind that it brought. There was a small stream nearby and in the depths of its narrow but deep pools lurked mountain trout, blackfish and yabbies.. a crustacean delight. Brumbies were heard at night and smelled by day but rarely seen. These wild horses were sometimes hunted by horse traders and high country cattlemen for their strength and agility. They had bred naturally over two hundred years from stock escaped from the early pioneers and miners that came into the district to seek their fortunes. There were neither horses nor camels in Australia before the coming of the white man. The plain below the hut was dotted with large rounded granite boulders that had been shoved and dragged by the glacial ice flows during the last ice-age, ending some 14000 years ago. The trees and undergrowth were filled with birds and humming insects. An occasional hare or rabbit was seen and the father would set traps for these.

The boy grew close to his rough parent on these trips watching him hunt and cook simple meals over the fire always accompanied by large mugs of tea. In the evening his father would lace his tea with a generous swish of rum. He was not a singer of songs but could play a few tunes on a harmonica. Before settling down to sleep the boy would stare into the red embers of the crackling fire listening to the tunes on his father's harmonica. The man could narrate a story but was not much of a conversationalist. But this suited the boy.

The Cobberas number 2 was a place that the boy had visited only a couple of times when the man had a break of four to five days. It was an arduous task to get there and the boy had to carry his share of what was necessary in the way of blankets and victuals. Sometimes by way of a large valley named the Playgrounds and sometimes by way of a more direct but steeper route skirting what was called Moscow Peak. The boy was almost certain to attain a distant view of brumbies in this area. A flash of gold might appear in the form of a proud and beautiful dog. This was the mountain dingo (alpine dingo) whose winter coat was indeed the texture of gold. In a cliff face just below the peak, his father showed him a small cave that penetrated the rock by three to four metres, sufficient shelter for three persons or more at a squeeze. The top of the mountain was open meadowland of rich grass interspersed with a blanket of wildflowers. Snow gums huddled together tightly in patches to give shelter from the wind. A spring formed just below the land bridge between the aforementioned peaks where the father loved to make their camp. A clump of larger trees grew here, the trunks twisted and tortured by many seasons of snow and freezing winds. Silver, green and pink ribbons of bark hung down together giving delightful colour. A wilder scene one could not find. At night seated close to the fire, a sea of twinkling points of light shone overhead. The current of the Milky Way swept across the deep black sky with prominent constellations vivid to the eye such as the great warrior Orion and his dog Canis. Some stars twinked red, orange or a play of colours rapidly flashing alternatively. Fire flies flew past and an occasional meteor raced across the sky. The boy's heart was delighted by these heavenly shows. The night air was always very cold here and the boy pulled his coat tightly around his body as he edged closer to the roaring blaze. His father started to tell him a story:

"You know the cave son that we visited on our way? Well it was well known to the local tribe here abouts, the Ja'atnegarra. They would come up to what we call the Quombat flat to hunt the grey kangaroo each summer. A young boy would be sent off to this place alone to become a man. He must survive with his woomera (spear) and boomerang for many days before returning to the main encampment as part of his coming of age. The cave was reserved for emergency if snow descended suddenly and the boy could squeeze in and light a fire. The weather is always unpredictable with snow storms appearing in the middle of summer."

The boy listened attentively.

"Well one time in early autumn when the tribe usually prepare to descend to the lower forests and plains, a chieftain sent his first son on his trial. Being late in the season a wicked storm blew in from the south and much snow was deposited on these mountains. The son wandered about and soon became cold and frightened. On seeing a golden dingo, he followed the animal to his lair.. the very cave of which we speak. It is said that the boy scrambled into the cave and lay alongside the dingo for three days and was unharmed by the dog but managed to keep warm enough. After the storm passed the boy descended to the Quombat flat only to meet his wretched and bemoaning father that thought he had lost his son due to his own foolishness. The chieftain hugged his son with tears of joy on their reunion. From that day the tribe never hunted or killed the golden mountain dingo but held it in high esteem for saving the chieftain's son. How true the story is remains unknown, but it has been passed down for many generations among the local tribe as part of their folk lore. Unfortunately they no longer live in these hills and their former culture and way of life is gone forever."

The boy slumbered and dreamed of the chieftain's son snug in his cave with the dingo whilst the man played a few sad tunes on his harmonica. Mars followed Jupiter across the night sky and all was well with the microcosmic world of the boy and his dad. Or was their world cosmic and greater than that of most?

Stream

The Ghost Stream is a moderate water course that converges with the MacMillan River some 30 kilometres south of Rushing Creek. It flows through heavily timbered hills and experiences no open country from its source to its convergence. Gold was discovered along its course in the 1850's and a small settlement, Sovereign, of tents and shanties grew where the gold was most plentiful. Some mines were also opened up and machinery brought in by bullock. MacIntyre claimed that his great great grandfather was a baker cum prospector and set up a small oven and baker's shop at the camp with his wife. A water wheel and small battery were also set up and the camp survived for a couple of decades. It was an exceedingly secluded spot.

The boy fossicked about looking for bottles or valuables that remained. He found an English half-penny with a youngish Queen Victoria stamped on one side and Britannia on the other; some tobacco tins as well as a complete whiskey bottle, squarish and of deep green glass. There remained channels and walls of stone to do with the plant, stone chimneys, broken glass and pottery.

The man quietly fished, wading up the stream and flicking his line ahead. Two sizeable rainbow trout were caught and the pair feasted on these for their lunch, the blue smoke of the camp fire twirling and curling upwards between very tall and sturdy gums. The man took out some tobacco and rolled it in a paper, licked the edge and adeptly placed the cigarette between his lips all with his single left hand. Taking a small stick radiating from the embers he lit the fag and leaned back against a white granite boulder and gazed up at the foliage overhead. Green and magenta flashes of a group of parakeets swooped just above his head.

"What you got there son?" he enquired of the boy.

Father and son partake lunch by the Ghost Stream

"Jest a few pieces an' a bottle dad.. oh an' this here halfpenny with a Queen's head on it!"

He passed the coin to the man who spat on it and rubbed it against his trousers.

"Hmm, 1853. That's a good find son. We have a few Chinese coins from up Castle way with square holes, but this is the first of the old money. Might be worth something but better to keep don't you think?"

A broad smile beamed over the boy's face.

"Yeah, not gonna give this'un away."

Just then a dragon lizard leapt from the water and raced up a slanting tree trunk on the bank just a few metres away. He froze and did not move again for many minutes. A large bluish dragon fly hovered over the rippling waters. The light played on the small rocks and rounded stones on the bed of the stream, mainly greys and blues but with some white quartz and green granite. Fronds of ferns swished back and forth like conductors' batons at allegro pace.

After a snooze under the midday sun with the breeze and insects buzzing about, both man and boy went back to their earlier pastimes, the boy fossicking and the man fishing for trout. When the man had bagged three more good fish, they called it a day and followed the walking track down stream back to the old utility. The forest was warm but not unpleasantly hot under a canopy of tall ribbon gum, ash and river gum. The walk took them a couple of hours past small waterfalls, scurrying lizards, a black snake and constantly accompanied by a cacophony of bird calls, pipes and whistles. No other soul was met along the track. The boy plodded along behind the man, proudly carrying his leather satchel with the day's finds. The man carried his rod and basket containing the evening's dinner. Trout for two successive meals mattered not. It was a simple luxury and Mrs Mack and the younger brother and sister would be thrilled at the treat.

The engine of the old car burst into life and the pair carefully wended their way back up the twisting highway to their home at the mill town of Rushing Creek. A rouge sky with ribbons of pink and blue overhead reminded the boy of the colourful fish in his dad's basket and the ribbons of bark hanging down from the giant trees along the stream.

Queen Victoria Half Penny- "the old money"

Family

The MacIntyre family had migrated from Scotland's West Coast at the beginning of the 1820's or at least, to be concise, two brothers Angus and John. The parents had been crofters and came from a line of Jacobites, both bringing extreme problems and hardship to the family. The local Laird, one James Kennedy, had cruelly forced the family off their small holding in Ayrshire on the western side of Scotland. The proud son Angus had had an altercation with this local Laird so he decided to travel with his younger brother to a new land to seek new opportunities, freeing himself of this unsentimental and cruel feudalistic thane. He had read in the newspaper (Ayr and Wigtownshire Courier) that land was freely available for would-be farmers arriving at Port Jackson in the new colony of New South Wales. They paid their ship's passage firstly out of Glasgow, then via Liverpool to Southampton. Here for the fare of two pounds and nineteen shillings each, they joined the convict ship 'Countess of Harcourt' carrying mainly female convicts from various parts of England. Sailing via the Cape of Good Hope, across the Indian Ocean, the Southern Ocean and on past Van Diemen's Land, they eventually disembarked at Port Jackson in July 1821.

Not all those barques, clippers and sail ships made it safely to the new world. In August 1843 the emigrant ship Cataraque, some 800 tons and carrying a complement of almost four hundred souls, met a gale in Bass Strait on her one hundredth day out from Liverpool, England. The ship was swept onto rocks and over a period of twenty four hours completely broke up. Eight crew (excluding the captain) plus a single passenger, one Solomon Brown of thirty years, were the only survivors. Solomon lost his wife and four daughters. The Cataraque, captained by one C.W.Finlay, was headed for the colony at Port Phillip (now Melbourne). What became of poor Solomon?

Whilst on the voyage out, Angus fell head over heels with a convict girl named Eliza Stubbs, a farm labourer and milking maid from Kent. Her crime was that she had stolen half a round of cheese from her employer, a rough and uncouth farmer, in order to adequately feed herself and her parents during the winter. For this crime she was given a sentence of transportation to Australia for seven years. On arrival at Port Jackson, the dear girl was newly pregnant and on payment of two pounds Angus was permitted to take Eliza for his wife, saving her from a hard existence in the penal colony. Eliza was sixteen years old. She gave birth to a son Angus Hamish the following year. For a further ten pounds, the brothers were permitted to take up a pastoral lease of 600 acres some two hundred miles to the south west. Starting with four horses, a single ram and a dozen ewes, some tools and camping equipment, they set off to build a crude house and sheep farm in the region that is now known as the Southern Tablelands. This was accomplished after many years of hard labour. Unfortunately, the younger brother John caught lock-jaw (tetanus) and died within two years of their arrival.

The son Angus Hamish did not show particular interest in farming and at the early age of seventeen, made his way back to Sydney where he sailed by packet to the new colony of Port Phillip and Melbourne. He met a bonny lass named Jane Elizabeth Coulter, a dairy maid from Surrey, England that had accompanied her parents to farm in the new colony. After marrying in 1838, they decided to set up a small bakery in Geelong to the south west of Melbourne. They had three able sons Gerald, Roy and William. The business was steady and they remained in Geelong for a further fourteen years.

From here in 1854 the family travelled by coach to the Ballarat gold fields. Angus knew little about the techniques of gold mining (having lived on a farm and later, been apprenticed for a short term to a baker in Goulburn, New South Wales) but soon teamed up with a Scottish immigrant, one Raglan McMaster and managed to eke out enough of the yellow metal to buy himself clothes, a humble cottage and a couple of good horses

However after a few years Angus yearned to travel again. He had heard of gold being found in East Gippsland and so the family packed up and sailed from Williamstown to the Gippsland Lakes area. Another three days by wagon brought them to the Ghost Stream. Here they set up camp, looking for nuggets by day and baking bread by night. The family survived eight years, slowly saving enough money to move on to a better life.

Eventually the family moved to Hobart, Tasmania in 1863, where the bakery business was at its most successful. Their three sons went into various trades. The eldest boy Gerald became a tree feller and worked in the forest cutting specialised timbers for boat building, notably Huon Pine. Huon Pine, much sought after for boat building, is one of the slowest-growing and longest-living plants in the world and can grow to an age of 3000 years or more. And so a branch of the family became associated with the timber industry both in Tasmania and later, in the ranges close to the North East of Melbourne. Roy carried on in the bakery business with his parents and William became a fisherman, working boats in Bass Strait until lost at sea with his boat in a storm in 1869 at age twenty years.

Two MacIntyres of the Hobart family (sons of Roy Wallace MacIntyre) fell in the Great War; Robert in the Dardanelles and Henry in Flanders. They were 24 and 18 years respectively. Angus survived. Was it the luck of his name?

Dan MacIntyre was born at Woodend, Victoria in 1932, the youngest of five children to Angus and Louisa MacIntyre (as aforementioned, Angus being the son of Roy MacIntyre). His eldest brother Michael was killed in Greece in 1941 during the war, serving with the Australian 2/3rd Field Regiment. His other brother, Hamish, remained at Woodend and the two sisters Felicity and Elizabeth, after marriage, lived in various parts of Melbourne. Dan met Mary at the Royal Melbourne Show in 1954. After a brief romance and a lot of travelling back and forth between Woodend and Williamstown where Mary's family lived, the couple married at the Holy Trinity Anglican Church Nelson Place, Williamstown in December 1955. The boy was born in Carlton in 1957 followed by a younger brother, then a sister three years and six years later respectively. The family lived happily at Woodend whilst there was still timber to be had in the forests about and Dan was a regular member of the community in the small town. He had worked in the mill more or less since the age of fourteen and knew pretty much all the basic jobs. But he was merely a hand and did not have a skill such as saw doctor, electrician, engineer or mechanic.

Earlier, at age fifteen, Dan had been involved with a group of men that had the idea of travelling to Melbourne's wealthier Eastern suburbs at weekends and burgle houses. Dan was foolish to become involved in this buffoonery as the family had hit some bad luck and needed some ready cash. On Dan's first expedition into the world of crime, he was caught by an enlightened police that were in waiting for the band. He served only eighteen months but it had destroyed his chances of respect and secure employment. After his release, he tried his hand at fishing in Bass Strait until almost drowned. He returned to the mill at Woodend.

Thus it was that Dan and his young family moved to Rushing Creek in 1963 where the local timber mill was working at full capacity and was finding it difficult to obtain a full complement of workers. Dan commenced on a much lower wage and worked long hours on the docking bench. But it was at least a new start and the mill provided accommodation for his family. The school was adjacent to the mill and it seemed a pretty little town; close to the mountains and good trout streams… maybe they could be happy here!

WWI and WWII service medals

Overleaf: MacIntyre Family Tree (1792 - 2010)

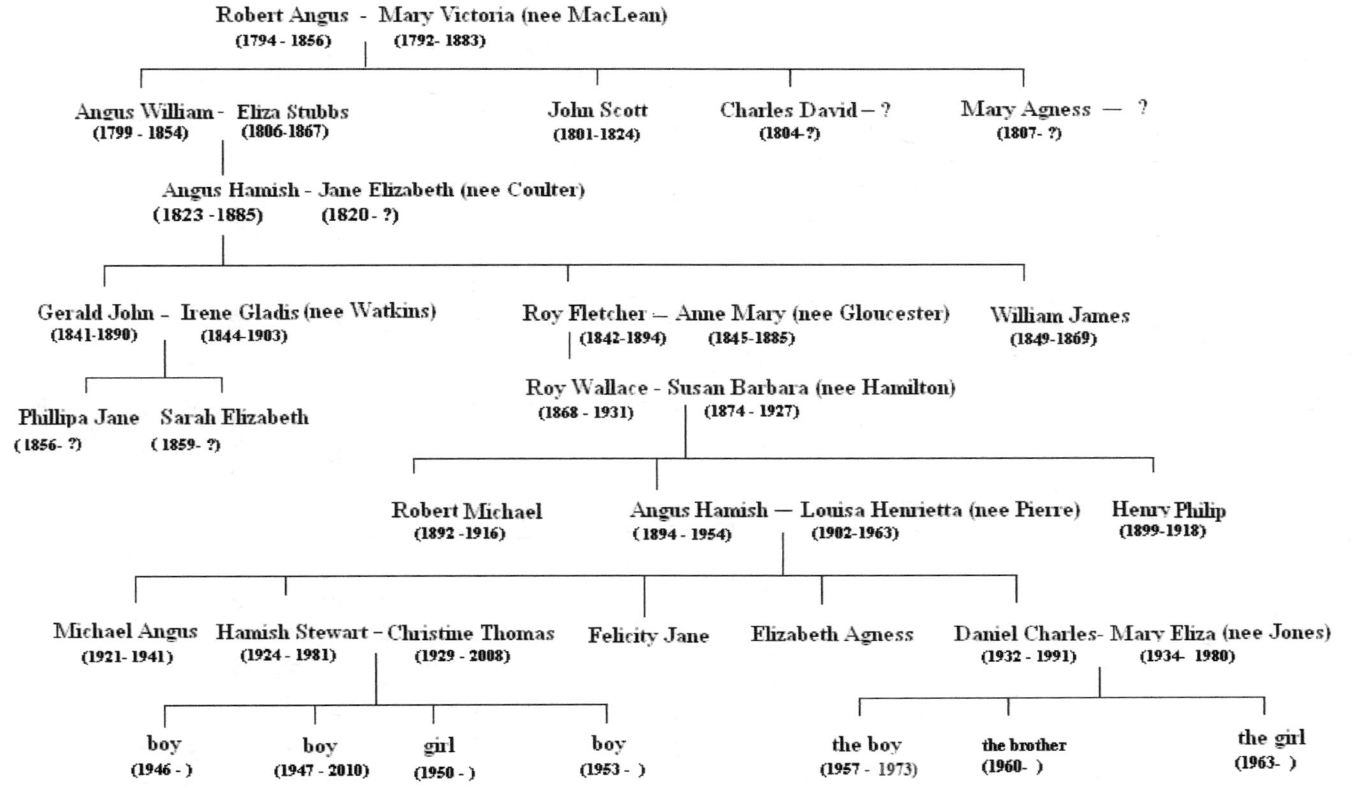

Robert Angus - Mary Victoria (nee MacLean)
(1794 - 1856) (1792- 1883)
Angus William - Eliza Stubbs
(1799 - 1854) (1806-1867)
John Scott
(1801-1824)
Charles David – ?
(1804-?)
Mary Agness — ?
(1807- ?)
Angus Hamish - Jane Elizabeth (nee Coulter)
(1823 -1885) (1820 - ?)
Gerald John – Irene Gladis (nee Watkins)
(1841-1890) (1844-1903)
Roy Fletcher – Anne Mary (nee Gloucester)
(1842-1894) (1845-1885)
William James
(1849-1869)
Phillipa Jane
(1856- ?)
Sarah Elizabeth
(1859- ?)
Roy Wallace - Susan Barbara (nee Hamilton)
(1868 - 1931) (1874 - 1927)
Robert Michael
(1892 -1916)
Angus Hamish — Louisa Henrietta (nee Pierre)
(1894 - 1954) (1902-1963)
Henry Philip
(1899-1918)
Michael Angus
(1921- 1941)
Hamish Stewart – Christine Thomas
(1924 - 1981) (1929 - 2008)
Felicity Jane
Elizabeth Agness
Daniel Charles- Mary Eliza (nee Jones)
(1932 - 1991) (1934- 1980)
boy
(1946 -)
boy
(1947 - 2010)
girl
(1950 -)
boy
(1953 -)
the boy
(1957 - 1973)
the brother
(1960-)
the girl
(1963-)

Confusion

The boy had left school and wondered what he would do next. The brief experience in the shearing shed had led him to the only real and practical alternative.. a job at the timber mill. At first he was given simple tasks like keep an eye on the dust burner and feed it off-cuts so it did not extinguish; assist with dragging away bark from the flitch cutting area so workers would not trip. He was not placed on any machine; being just fifteen years, the company' insurance would not cover a junior. He would however accompany others on machines just to see what was required and get the feel of the place. The Russian in the engineering shop was perhaps the only man that had any time for the boy, welcoming him into his workshop for a chat or even to give him some small task:

"Over there are some spanners, screwdrivers and grips, now see if you can strip this small engine down so's we can have a look at the inside!" -and the boy would attempt the task of taking the engine apart under the watchful eye of the Russian. The man, already in his late fifties, wore a kindly expression under his peaked cap. His blue eyes always twinkled and he showed patience with the boy. Not so for the other workers at the mill. Whenever some machine broke down he would always cuss at their stupidity, particularly at the operator for his sloppy and careless handling of the machine. The fault was always with the operator:

"I've told you many times before you must start the machine this way. Always check the oil, check the tension on the band and reset it to within the tolerance like this! These are simple instructions which you just don't seem to be able to follow and you wonder why it is broken down!"

The Russian could never accept natural wear and tear and was consistently gruff with the workers. But he was a highly skilled albeit unqualified engineer and the management and everyone tolerated his abuse, knowing that he could fix just about anything. At weekends he had a stream of locals with everything from tractors to motorbikes and chainsaws pleading for him to “jest have a look to get the buggar goin’ again!” And the Russian always found it hard to say no! So the boy began to learn a lot from the engineer although this was not his set task from the foreman.

Not all the hands liked Dan, but after his accident were less inclined to pass comment on the boy. However, the odd one or two were mean and would send him off on some impossible errand:

“There is a leak at the reservoir, could you go check it out?” or “I need a 32 inch spanner, would you go fetch one from the Russian’s workshop and be snappy ‘bout it!” or “Go down to the corner store and fetch a couple o’ gallons of defrosting paint to keep these planks free of frost before we cut them up!”

But the boy was not so dumb and would use these opportunities to spend more time with the Russian. On enquiring “did you get the paint?” he would sardonically reply “oh yes, the storeman said there was a big demand from most of the farmers and so it is on back order.. won’t be in for a couple of weeks!” which of course amused everyone including the boy and the Russian.

“Don’t worry ‘bout those dumbheads” he would scoff, “most of ‘em wouldn’t know their arse from their elbow. You just stick with me and do your work here.”

As said, the boy had never been a keen participant in team sports such as football. However, on occasion he would venture to the footy ground on a Saturday morning and watch a game. As the girls would be playing netball he would spend a greater part of his time there. He had a special reason for doing so; his distraction was a slim young lass named Bridget of fair complexion and golden locks, usually tied in a pony tail.

Bridget currently attended the local school and was the daughter of a sheep farmer that owned one of the largest properties in the region. One might almost describe them as 'aristocracy' if such a thing existed in Australia. The boy had always had a soft spot in his heart for this comely country girl. She spoke with a more educated accent which set her apart a little from the town girls but she was an active participant in sport such as netball and horse riding and was skilled enough to be accepted. The boy had made small efforts to be close to her at school and had even given her small gifts of things he had found in the bush. A special piece of quartz or amethyst from Quombat, and even a slither of gold he had panned on Rushing Creek near Ah Fat corner. Bridget had always accepted his gifts and touched his hand along with a caring smile. Being a bit of an outsider herself, she had an affinity for this strange and quiet boy. Of course, her mother would never approve of any boyfriend-girlfriend relationship, but Bridget definitely felt something for the boy, even if she appeared guarded to the community around her. She tendered his gifts in places of importance in her bedroom at the rambling farmhouse and would handle them lovingly on occasion.

"Where did you get that crystal Bridget?" her mum once asked.

"Oh, just from a friend at school mum" she replied coyly.

Bridget was always aware when the boy was watching the netball game on Saturday mornings and she would excel herself for him.

At the end of the football season there would always be a ball at the Mechanics Institute hall in the town, a combined affair between the football and netball clubs. There would be a band from Maintown and dancing, followed by a meal and awards for the year's best and fairest players. And so it was that the boy attended with his parents. During the progressive folk dance the boy got to hold Bridget for a few twirls before moving on to the next partner. But she made the best of the opportunity quickly whispering into his ear:

"Ask me for a dance when the waltz starts!"

The boy was excited and later in the evening sure enough the band commenced to play some waltzes. But before then an amusing incident occurred to the mirth of all present.

The town drunk Jonny Patel was there in clean shirt, black trousers and polished shoes. He remained mostly at a corner table with a dark-haired gypsy looking lady greatly overexposed with lipstick and rouge, a long purple frilly dress and probably in her mid-fifties. At last they got up to partake of the first waltz. They were more than a little unsteady. Only a half-dozen couples had commenced to dance when in came a very tall and robust horsey woman, cussing and looking about the hall. On espying the staggering couple at the centre of the floor she walked directly to them, ripped the wig from the woman, hurled it towards the band all the while screaming at the top of her voice vulgar adjectives at the couple. Some burley men quickly removed her from the building, including the town policeman dressed in mafia style suit and tie. Apparently Jonny had two women on the go, one a local and one that would visit from Geelong from time to time!

After the kafuffle had died down, the boy nervously approached the table where Bridget was seated with her younger brother. Her parents were already dancing and the floor was packed.

"May I have the honour of this dance" he stumbled.

"Why certainly young man" replied Bridget with colour in her cheeks and naughty smile. She had tippled a little from her father's wineglass and was in a confident mood. The couple held each other close but spoke no words. Each could feel a warmth pass between their young bodies and the boy knew at once that he loved this rare and elegant flower of a girl. She was wearing a sleek white dress over her slim form with a blue sash presented earlier in the evening for her netball award as the 'best junior for the season'. She also had a white band in her hair and matching white patent high heeled shoes. The boy then plucked up enough courage to say:

"I want to kiss you."

"Not here, another time" she whispered in his ear and squeezed him a little tighter to show her approval of the demand. The parents twirled past and the mother gave her daughter a strong look of disapproval. Her father just winked and gave a little smile.

"I will ride my horse to the river tomorrow morning about ten. We could meet at the Willows, OK?"

"Sure" the boy said.

Soon the music was over and people commenced leaving the ancient hall, with its polished timber frames of honours' lists of past councillors and club presidents to stare down at an empty floor. The boy wandered home dreamily thinking about the morrow's meet with his new love.

The day was cloudy with a hint of rain and the breeze was swift as it blew across the river flats stretching from north to south of the village. The boy was sitting watching the water drift past in small ripples, coils and wavelets. He perceived a trotting close by and Bridget arrived on her dappled grey pony, its mane and tail neatly plaited. She was wearing her full riding gear: polished boots with jodhpurs, neat chocolate suede jacket and riding hat. She carried a small leather whip in her right hand. Adroitly alighting from her steed and tying him to a willow branch she approached the boy. His whole soul and being was trembling to see his princess, but the girl was confident and taking his hand merely said "Hi!" They looked steadily into each others eyes and slowly but surely their lips met. It was a slow and long embrace.

The boy and Bridget at the willows

“You know I have to go away next Feb?” she said in a pitiful soft voice and looking away.
“No, why is that?”
“My mum and dad are sending me to Pressy Girls in Melbourne.. it was mum’s old school. But we have ‘til Christmas and all the summer” she said convincingly; and further “we cannot meet often but we can find ways yes?”
The boy was both happy yet confused. He had found a love but it was threatened before it had begun.
“I will come home for term holidays and we can write” she reassured pressing his hand in hers. The new willow shoots waved in harmony with the heavy yellow blossom of wattle. Dragon flies hovered over the rushes at the edge of the stream. They embraced again and the boy’s heart was filled to bursting. After half an hour she said:
“I must get back. I’m sorry you are no longer at school. We can meet here next Sunday. Maybe we can swim if the weather is warmer, but I will have to bring my brother, so no kissing.”
But it was more than the boy could have hoped for. The following week dragged by and the boy moved about his work in a dream. Even the Russian could see that he was possessed with some thought or other.

On the following Sunday it was a little cold for swimming but the sun was warm enough and they enjoyed their time together. The girl had brought her younger brother and a picnic basket with sandwiches, cake and homemade lemonade. Whilst the younger brother was mooching about poking at lizards with a stick they managed to exchange a few quick kisses. Unfortunately the brother told his mum about the ‘boy from the mill’ so that it was difficult for them to meet after that. But meet they did despite the mother’s warning:

“I don’t want you to see that boy. His father is a criminal you know. He is a bad influence and you are not to see him again.”

Bridget’s father did not chide his daughter or try to restrict her in any way. He loved her dearly and trusted her sensibility.

“You must show me the Castle Mine one day dad- I hear it is very interesting.”

“That can be arranged, I’m sure your brother would love to go along.”

Of course by more than coincidence, the boy was waiting for the party. The father was impressed by the young man’s knowledge of the old battery and equipment that was used to process the ore. The boy gave a continuous commentary about everything and was able to answer questions by the grazier.

“Were there any dangers to the miners and workers in this plant?”

“Oh yes” answered the boy confidently. “When the ore is roasted, the gas arsine is formed which is most poisonous and some workers were overcome by the toxic fumes. There were also accidents by falling rocks and cave-ins as witnessed by the graves in the Castle cemetery. Some were in their teens when killed.”

Bridget was very proud of the boy but gave no indication to her father that she had feelings for him.. or so she thought.

Later that night at home her father looked seriously at her across the dinner table and enquired:

“Bridget, was that your young man we met at the Castle Mine site today?”

“Father, I don’t know what you mean” she replied with a hot rouge spreading across her cheeks. Her dad smiled and looked at the ceiling with a short polite cough. He realised at once the truth.

The boy did not see Bridget as often as he wished over the summer. He had to work and the parents had taken her away on holiday to Bali for a couple of weeks. She wrote a couple of postcards and they did spend the odd day together. But pretty soon February rolled round and they each had to face their parting. They met briefly under their willow tree the last Sunday morning. The boy had saved his humble earnings and presented Bridget with a silver friendship ring.

"I won't be permitted to wear it in school, but I will keep it with my things and wear it when I can escape for shopping or excursions."

"I will think of you every day" said the boy. "Please don't forget to write me."

She gave him a lock of her hair and they kissed more tenderly than ever. Bridget could not hold back her tears. She gave the boy one last small kiss on his forehead and said in the faintest of words:

"I love you James"… and then she was gone.

Unbeknown to each, Bridget's mother ensured that any mail to or from Bridget at the privileged school was to be forwarded directly to her at the sheep and cattle station at Rushing Creek, an censoring act of cruelty.

The boy walked out to his favourite place on the upper reaches of the Creek. He could hear the newcomer hammering then busying himself with his shovel, mixing cement to lay more stones on his walls. Eventually he moved on to the hole in the steep sand cliff and quietly called out:

"Akimitsu, Akimitsu, are you there?"

After a long wait, he heard a shuffling in the tunnel and then his old friend appeared at the tunnel entrance.

"I have brought you some tender beef, tea and sugar. How have you been?"
"Oh, Akimitsu not so well these days. Come, come, we shall have tea together."
The boy followed the soldier into his lair and together in the cool they sipped mint tea and home brewed nettle wine. The boy told the soldier about his new love and her departure. Tears appeared in the old man's eyes.
"Ha, I know your sad feeling. I miss my little Etsu so much that my heart wants to explode. But you have a chance. You must be stlong, patient and place your tlust in this love; then all will be well for you and it will also bling much pleasure for me."
The two sat in silence for many minutes as each thought about their own lives and their present predicaments.
"But her family is very rich. They will never accept their daughter attached to one as humble as me. I really have no chance and perhaps I should wake up to reality!"
"There is always hope my son, always hope. And the heavens move in stlange ways. No one can pledict future events, we can only play and tly our best to fulfil our dleams. Do not be like me. I have sat here in this cave most of my life and let my dleams slip away."
The soldier then started to wail a little intermittently calling:
"Oh my Etsu, oh my Etsu!"
"I should go home; I have an early start in the morning. I will bring you more meat next time."
"Take this small jar of honey, a small gift flom Akimitsu to his dear flend" said the soldier, pressing the jar into the boy's hands.
With that the boy left.

Sea

The father of the boy also loved to fish at the seashore or from a small boat on one of the lakes or inlets next to the ocean. It was only an hour and a half to the Lakes and during the summer months the family would go on a weekend excursion, camping overnight next to the salt and sand. Occasionally, they would venture as far as Cann River then head south to the wild coast of the Thurra River where they would spend four or more days fishing, swimming and wandering the beach to their hearts' content. Again, the man would sometimes go alone with just the boy at his side.

The lakes and inlets would provide them with tasty flathead and prawns when in season. They would row out into the dark with a small gas lamp and lower a broad net. After several minutes they would quickly hoist up the net to receive God's plentiful reward of a kilogram of prawns or more. These days there are many more fishermen and fewer prawns but in the early 1970's there were ample. Mum would boil them up in a billycan and the family then sit around the campfire feasting on the deliciously fresh crustaceans. The man would have a couple of bottles of beer, usually a Melbourne Bitter or a Carlton Draft to "assist with me deegestion!"

At the beach next to the mouth of the Thurra they would fish for sea trout, rock cod and other seasonal fish. At Hicks Point, they would search the small bays for pipits, scallops and abalone- a leathery shellfish much sought after for the export market to Japan. The man showed the son the many mounds of empty shells once collected by the native peoples of the area over thousands of years; middens they are called. Around these can be found shards and flakes of white quartz, interspersed with the carbon from ancient campfires. These were the discarded pieces from the making of spear heads for fishing. On a sandy cliff face, one could detect many layers deeper down of the same mixture of sea-shell, quartz and charcoal going back tens of thousands of years.

This point was the first sighting of Eastern Australia by Captain James Cook aboard the barque Endeavour on 20 April 1770 and named after the first officer, Lieutenant Hicks. (Cape Hicks was later renamed Cape Everard). A lighthouse stands high on the rocky point with two homes close by for the keepers and their families. The houses are surrounded by stone walls of the same ochre granite that the lighthouse and dwellings are built, all mined on the point.

Walking westwards past a shipwreck and a couple of small bays the boy and his father reached the beach again and camped. Fishing in the shallows the boy caught a Port Jackson shark. Meanwhile the father had waded out close to a rocky outcrop and managed to catch a few rock cod.

"Well my son, that will make a nice dinner fer us, but you know this species is now protected- next time throw him back!"

The father and son enjoyed a wonderful feed of boneless fresh fish that night and under the stars the boy once more was entreated by his father's tales:

"As a younger man not yet seventeen years, I fished in Bass Strait mainly for tuna but also for shark and whatever we could get. With a heavy load 'n' our wells being filled to the brim, we were headed back to Apollo Bay when a vicious storm blew out of the South West. Instead of wearing it out at sea, the captain decided to make a run for it to port. The boat was a fifty foot Tasmanian smack, broad in the beam and of about thirty ton unladen and thirty four ton laden with fish. She carried an eight cylinder Gardner diesel engine and was all made of one inch spotted gum with a straight red gum keel and Queensland celery decking.

In Bass Strait

We pushed along with foam leaping right over the top of the cabin where four of us clustered all a'praying and a'fearing for our lives. All the while this great petrel soared above us… he was most similar to a sooty but definitely a petrel with a wingspan the same as the height of a man! At dusk we could see the lamp and were about six mile out to sea when she heaved around broadside and rolled over like a rolling pin in the stream. Well, we was done for then. Suddenly I was in the water and the smack belly up like a giant whale. There were lines flailing about in the water which waz boiling like a billy of porridge an' I manages to get a hold of one of these. I could hear another man yelling and screaming, but in the dark I could not see him. "Swim towards the ship" I calls out many times. But soon after there was nought to be heard but the wind and waves beating against the hull. For my luck the well boards 'n hatches were not so strongly attached an' when she rolled, she dumped the whole cargo of four days fishing back to the briny. But I should be grateful, as this prevented the old girl from a'sinkin' an' eventually I was able to drag myself in closer. I hung on for mercy all that night an' half the next day 'fore I was hauled out of the sea by another trawler that had dragged her heels out to sea and was saved. An' you know, that petrel was still a'circling the boat right up to I was hauled out the sea... like some guardian angel she was, watching o'er me I swear! Your daddy was the only one alive from the crew, the rest never being seen again. The boat, the Merle she was called, was salvaged an' went on te fish 'til this very day, that well built she was! One of your great great uncles was a'taken in much the same way in those waters more then a hundert year ago! William his name was and he being only a lad o' twenty years. So I says to meself then.. 'Fishin' at sea is not the career for you Dan me lad!' and I never returned to it after that."

The boy loved to hear his dad tell of his experiences and other snippets of the MacIntyre family history.

Back on the bank next to the Thurra river one morning, the bacon being served up and ready to consume, a kookaburra swooped down and off again in one easy parabolic movement with a slice of bacon in its mouth.

"Gotta eat quick 'round here son else nature'll take it all away from you!" was all his dad remarked. Giant lizards slothed about the undergrowth under the bottlebrush and banksias, also looking for a chance to carry off something edible. The man took a small sip of rum.

"Essential for removing ticks my boy. Lot of ticks in this coastal bush!"

The boy liked to spend time alone in the giant sand dunes or fossicking along the shore picking up shells, starfish and dried cuttlefish for the pet cockatoo to peck at back home. He swam only on the calmest of days and even then was nervous in case a shark ventured in. Sometimes these waters were infested with jelly fish that would give an annoying sting, but not life threatening.

Eventually it was time to load up the old Holden and wend there way home. The boy was never certain which he loved the most: the shore, the mountain or the forest? He thought about this as he nodded off on the long journey home. There was no answer in any case. He loved those rare occasions to be with his dad. He loved it all and was happy to live in such a wonderful part of his country, Australia!

Community

The small village of Rushing Creek lies on broad river flats of the MacMillan River and was settled in the 1850's. The finding of gold in the region brought many migrants from a diverse number of countries including Europe, the Americas and Asia. Cattlemen had entered the region in the 1830's and two large stations appeared at that time, Nambra to the north east and Islay in the south. At that time these were considered extremely remote. Sydney was perhaps eighteen to twenty days away by horse and the new settlement at Melbourne best reached by ship. After the subsidence of the original surge of miners, small landowners started to farm the land and graze cattle and sheep. There were possibly two to three hundred aboriginals living in the entire area, moving into the hinterland during the summer months then receding to the coastal plains for the winter. It is most likely that some small groups remained in the Rushing Creek area all year round as there was sufficient open ground to guarantee fresh kangaroo and wallaby meat (Bun jirra gingee munje... big kangaroos go to that place!) By 1920 timber milling had commenced in the area. Whilst the ethnic mix was predominantly British (i.e English, Scottish, Welsh and Irish), there was also a sprinkling of Dutch, German, Italian and Chinese. To a lesser extent, Scandinavian and other central European origins can also be traced along with intermarriages with Aboriginals and New Zealand Maori. Sadly, the native population were driven out by disease, murder and forced rehabilitation. It is a topic that the local residents prefer not to discuss or claim to have no knowledge. However, historical researchers such as P.D.Gardner and others have provided convincing evidence that the above comments are true and need to be recognised by the greater community. Such practices were common in many parts of Australia during the 19th century. Tasmania contained several thousand natives in 1800. None pure bloods remain today. A final forced rehabilitation of the remnants of the Tasmanian aboriginal is to be found on Flinders Island. Today there is a community of half-bloods but no pure-bloods remain. The last of these now lie quietly in the cemetery on that island. A similar story lies with respect to the original peoples of Chatham Island off the east coast of New Zealand, all of which had disappeared by 1925. Aboriginal peoples of the Pacific and many other parts of the world suffered similar fates at the hands of Europeans, collectively known as the 'white man'.

Timber, cattle and sheep were the main commercial products of the area for the 20th century, with the demise of the gold era by the beginning of the First World War. The halcyon days of gold mining were between 1860 and 1910 which brought people and wealth to a remote and isolated community.

Firstly, the recession of the early 1930's followed by the 1939 bush fires and the Second World War all contributed to bring hardship to this community with the loss of sons and material wealth. But timber, cattle and sheep were slowly supplemented by a new earner.. the tourist. Better roads and the introduction of mains electricity in the late 1950's brought a new lease of life to the Shire.

The next influx of 'new people' occurred in the late 1960's and early 1970's with the 'back to earth movement', the flow of idealistic young families wishing to give up modern urban life for a simpler rustic life of the country. Dozens of these young people moved to build their own dwellings of mud, timber or stone. Many were professionals wishing a healthier life-style for their children. The movement was not unique to Australia but common in Western Europe as well as North America. Books like 'On Walden Pond' and 'The Greening of America' strongly influenced a generation that had grown up under the perceived threat of

Nuclear War. Self-sufficiency and survival were at the forefront of their thinking. Some locals welcomed the influx of a much needed commodity.. more children to fill the schools. Others were less tolerant of the long-haired hippy men all of whom were immediately labelled communists, drug addicts and loafers. This was unfair of course and slowly the community came to accept the newcomers and their eccentric ways. There was a revival of cinema and folk dancing as well as a full frontal collision of ideas on things such as conservation and farming techniques. The reward for both was that each learned from the other. The newcomers learned that rural life is essentially hard work. Some farmers did make efforts to conserve their land by planting wind breaks and trees along watercourses to reduce erosion. Others remained critical and made no changes at all. Despite all this, the modern farmer is more interested in sustainable farming (and therefore a constant income) than getting the best from the land here and now with no thought of tomorrow and future generations. Rural communities are exceedingly conservative. Even the computer was regarded with distrust for many years before advantages were seen sufficiently to change this view.

As mentioned in an earlier chapter, the village possessed just one grocery store, one butcher, a café, a bakery, a post office, a garage for petrol and vehicle servicing, a Bush nurse centre, a primary and secondary school combined. The State Forestry Commission and the State Electricity Commission each had a central office and work units based in the town. The main employer of course was the timber mill. Most of the surrounding farms were between 300 and 600 acres with three in the 2000 to 5000 acre size, described as stations.

There were many established clubs and societies such as football, netball, tennis, cricket, shooters, golf and bowls. The Country Women's Association ran meetings; there was a wool spinning club and a gardening club. Three churches held regular Sunday worship services albeit their attendances small. Dances were a fairly regular feature of the village. An agricultural and art show was held each Easter in Battery, as well as horse race days throughout the year. For the young people there was Scouting and Guides as well as pony club. Certainly the writer has missed many other activities and apologises to the community. Let's just say that for a small population, it was always a hive of activity.

And so it was that the boy met the newcomer as their separate worlds now intersected and collided into something new.

Doubt

The boy ventured out on his days off to the King Castle mine site. It was now April and the days were getting shorter and cooler. He had received but one letter from Bridget, posted in the city of Melbourne, although he wrote at least twice per week since her departure. Bridget's letter was fairly matter-of-fact though she did sign off with "I miss you".

The boy would bring things for Akimitsu such as newspapers, books and items of food for cooking. He had even managed to obtain a bottle of saké for the old man and with the 'White Stallion' on its label as of old! He was always very grateful and would insist they share a bowl of sukiyaki or rather just sit sipping tea together with a cup of one of his herbal wines and talk of the world outside and all the changes. The boy could see sadness in the man's face and a weariness that seemed to press harder on his fragile frame on each successive visit.

By late May, Akimitsu had developed a very bad cough which seemed to the boy very serious.

"You should come to town with me and see the doctor. He comes every Wednesday!"

"No, no… I have my honey and herbs. I will get better."

But the aging warrior did not get better. He became weaker and weaker until he could not leave his bed. The boy decided he must bring someone to see the soldier and soon. Perhaps his discovery would render him famous and earn him his fare home to his native Japan. The benefits now seemed to outweigh the prospect of continuous isolation for his friend.

He decided to take a day from work and bring the Bush nurse to the cave. On arriving at the cliff-face he asked the nurse to wait. She seemed perplexed and angry at having to walk through the bush to this place. The boy scrambled into the hole and made his way down the passage to Akimitsu's rooms. All was silent. The man lay stiff and motionless on his bed. It was clear to the boy that he had passed away. He had failed his friend. He had brought help too late. His heart filled with a mix of remorse, sadness and anger. On exiting he made up some excuse.

"Oh I am so sorry; my friend is not here anymore. I am so sorry to waste your time miss."

The nurse decided that the boy was whacko, playing some practical joke maybe to distract her for some reason. The nurse made her way back to her car leaving the boy in the bush. A light drizzle began to fall. The boy just sat and pondered his loss of a friend, one of the few he had. He sat and wept; but the sound of his voluminous tears was washed by the soft singing of the little stream. Embracing his sedulous character, he was now determined to keep Akimitsu a secret.

With resolve, the boy went back to Akimitsu's room, covered the man with a sheet then started to bring rocks from outside to close off the right hand passage at the end of the wombat hole. He worked for much of the day sealing off the soldier's private den. Then he shovelled sand against the rocks so that the entrance would not be easily noticed. It was hard work but he felt satisfaction that he had maintained his friend's dignity.

Unbeknown to the boy far away in a village of Japan's Kyushu Island was a simple plaque with a list of a dozen names. An inscription said "Fallen Warriors of His Majesty's Imperial Forces 1933-1945". Akimitsu's name took its pride of place. A small spray of white flowers had been recently laid by a kimono clad thin beautiful woman of mature years. Her name was Etsu.

The MacIntyres depart Rushing Creek

The walls of the newcomer's house were taking shape and the skeletal timbers forming roof trusses had appeared. His two young sons played with their toy cars, trucks and bulldozers in the sand. The boy could distinctly hear their laughter and simulated engine sounds as they played. He passed quietly by and on home.

A few days later it was time for the family departure to their new life and home in Tasmania. The boy had decided to stay at the mill for a while and would move into Mrs Valera's house next door. The boy's mother gave him a hug with tears flooding down her cheeks.

"Don't worry mum, I'll be OK. I will join you all at Christmas. It'll pass soon enough" he said as cheerily as he could make himself. Dad shook his left hand and slapped his shoulder.

"Now do your work diligently son, save your money an' keep out o' trouble."

"Yes dad, I will."

A small tear welled up in his eyes at the final moment of departure. The family got into the old car and moved off. They intended to drive to Port Melbourne and take the ferry. Macintyre probably should not be driving with just one arm but he was a stubborn man.

"She'll be right. I can do almost as much with one as with two" he boasted. The Russian and Mitch were there and gave a titter at this comment.

"Well goodbye Dan and good luck, goodbye Mary".

Autumn melded into winter and the months were cold and dreary. The boy had much on his mind and had become more introverted than normal. He had had no response to his letters to Bridget and by mid June he had stopped writing to her. Change is a heavy burden on us all. Sometimes it brings new experiences and challenges that we rise to and eventually adjust. We embrace our new environment and situation and move on happily. But at times the soul finds it hard to adjust, particularly if we are unlucky and several calamities eclipse, weighing more than usual upon us. The Russian would try to attract the boy to the workshop for chats and give him some new project. But the boy had even begun to avoid his friendly overseer. He did his work like a robot. At tea breaks and lunch he would sit alone, introvert, deep in contemplation.

No one could foresee the consequence of all these effects on the heart of the boy. Just a little more care, a few friendly words, an invitation for camaraderie was probably all that was needed. Mrs V was good to the boy but she was a widower with three young children of her own to worry about.

One very cold August morning the boy did not appear for breakfast. Mrs Valera was concerned as the boy was not in his room and his shift was to start at 6 am. It was still dark, the sun's rays not yet having penetrated the sleepy village this winter morn. Frost lay on the fence palings, the grass and low garden shrubs. For some inexplicable reason the lady decided to venture into the garage alongside the house. It was mainly used for storing old furniture and there were boxes stacked against the walls, a workbench and a few tools. The place was covered in cobwebs. She switched the light on. Immediately she gasped and swooned. The boy was hanging from a crude makeshift noose and a bentwood chair, kicked away, lay on the deeply oil stained cement floor. The dear lady composed herself and went out of the back gate into the mill yard and called to some men smoking before the start of the shift.

The policeman and the nurse were called. The men had cut the boy down and laid him in his room upon his bed.

"Oh the dear soul, the poor boy, whatever made him do such a thing?" wailed Mrs V over and over. The men stood about and barely muttered. Everyone was in a state of shock.

"It'll go hard on Dan and Mrs Mac" said one of the men.

The nurse had already pronounced the boy dead. The policeman was slow to arrive.

"Nothing should have been disturbed. Who cut the boy down? I will have to record names on this account" he blurted nervously and with some authority. He was a young cop in his late twenties with not a great deal of experience in handling such a case. He was also new to the area.

"We couldn't just leave him hanging like that. It was undignified" one of the men bravely piped up.

"The law is the law and this could be a crime scene. You should have done nothing 'til I arrived!"

The men just shrugged their shoulders and slowly filtered out into the morning that was now upon the town with a rouge sky over the hills to the east. A whistle blew to mark the beginning of the shift.

The boy had written no note. No final words to his mum and dad giving a reason. He was just a few days away from turning sixteen years old.

Only Dan came back from Tasmania to bury his son at the small cemetery at Islay. There was the Anglican minister and about six other persons including the Russian, Mitch, Mrs Valera, Bridget's father and the Bush nursing sister. It was a short, pathetic and sad ceremony. Dan stayed in the pub, the Old Dover for the night, but was not seen in the bar. He went to bed early and was away on the bus the next morning. It was a dismal day with low and dense blue-black clouds rolling in from the west. As the bus passed the cemetery Dan looked out of the window. He could just catch a glimpse of a few flowers on the mound where his boy now lay. He cried loudly like a wounded animal with no thought for his personal dignity. He could not remember when he had last cried like this; probably not since he was a child. Apart from the driver, there were no other passengers on the bus that morning. It remained a cloudy and windy day. The trees moaned and swayed heavily as the bus wound its way down to Maintown some ninety kilometres away. Snow lay on the crests of the higher peaks. Dan shivered in his thin jacket. Soon he dozed off until sharply awakened by the driver.

"Here's the station Dan. Take care and express my sympathies to Mrs Mac."

Just a mumble formed on the man's lips as he alighted from the vehicle in a dreamlike state. He gave a short wave of his left hand and was gone.

The newcomer shivered as he mixed cement and poured the grey slop into wooden forms to make concrete bricks. He smoothed off the top of the moulds with his trowel then stood up and looked about the swaying trees and scrub. There was a faint wail high overhead as the mistletoe swayed back and forth. On looking down to the creek he thought he got a glimpse of the boy in his familiar blue raincoat. It seemed like there was a young soldier at his side of Asian appearance. The uniform was khaki and blended in with the background of blackwood and wattle. The newcomer squinted and rubbed his eyes to look again but he saw no one. Just a trick of the mind he thought. After all, he had heard of the sad ending of the boy from his wife, his wife who was now the new nurse in the town. The presence of the Japanese soldier was never discovered. His memory faded with the boy, both sleeping now and lying far from their kith and kin.

It is true that the boy was not ordinary and seen by most to be a loner. Despite the apparent loss of his girlfriend, he led a full and active life. In fact, one might describe his personality as being robust with a self-styled purpose and direction. There was no autopsy or post-mortem examination performed which one would have thought should be a matter of course for a suspected suicide of a young person. As the boy had left no note and gave no intention of such a sudden act there must remain an element of doubt as to whether this was in fact a suicide or a cleverly devised and enacted murder by some person or organised group. But then, what was their motive? Statistics show that many young Australian men do indeed take their own lives. But the suggestion and question remains… how many of these are assisted suicides i.e. murders? The newcomer and his wife, now the local community nurse, discussed this at length and dwelt on it for some while. But their lives were full and ongoing at a hectic pace. In time, the boy in blue raincoat was forgotten.

"Come ye back ye Cassilis crofter
Back to Uist your jewelled isle
Sailing home on the mainland packet,
Luff her sail….
Yes, sailing home on the mainland packet,
Luff her sail… "

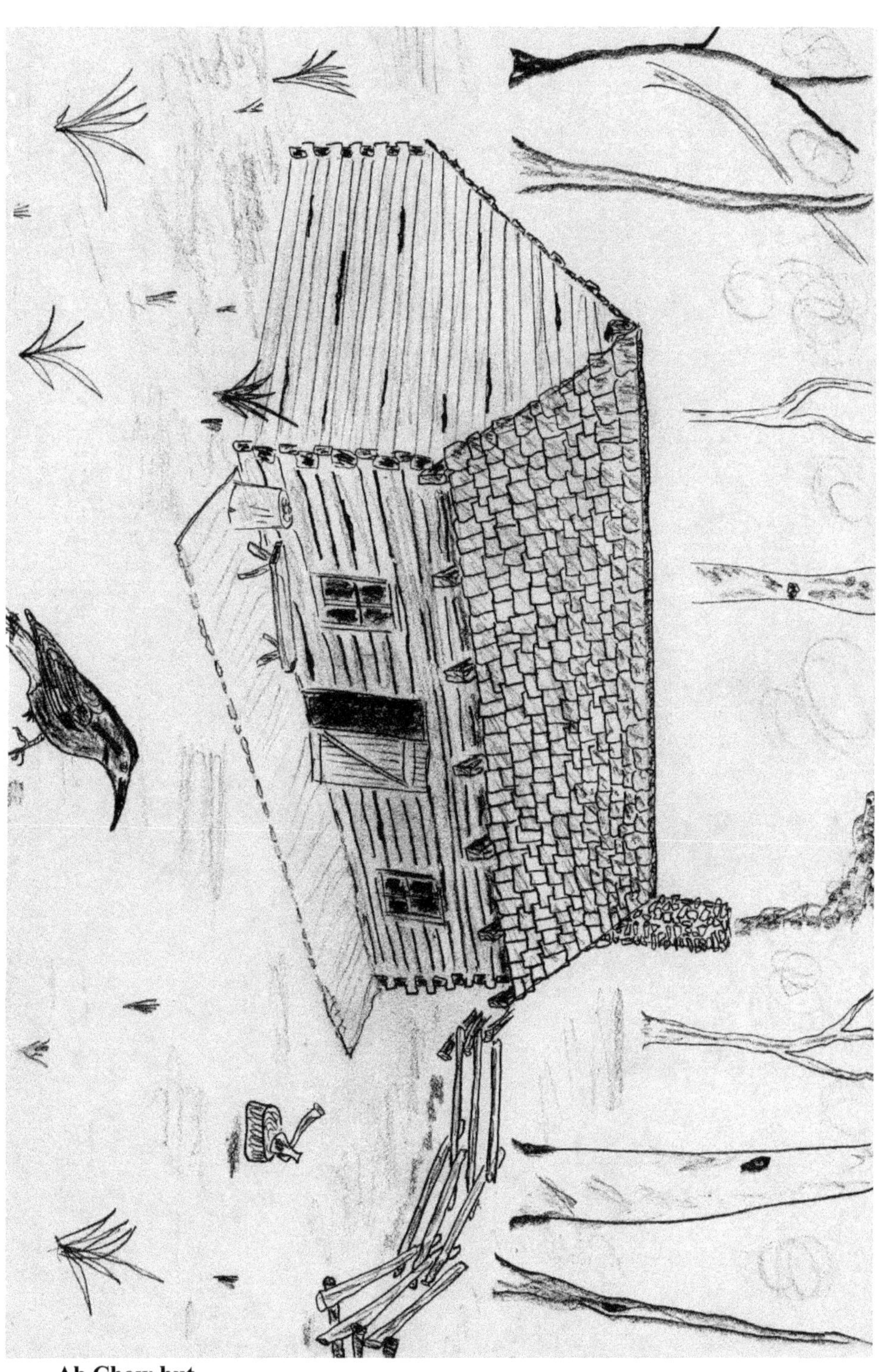

Ah Chow hut

Other Longership Titles:

They Came to the Shire

Chas Rose

ISBN 9780648702733

A compendium of owner builders that came to the Omeo Shire during the 1970s and 1980s.

The book describes how several families went about their individualised building project to create a home in this most beautiful part of Victoria- the mountains and forests of far East Gippsland.

Stonehouse One-

The Building of Brambly Cottage

Chas Rose

ISBN 9780987629852

A man escapes the hustle and bustle of the city to build his home among the mountains and forests of south east Australia. Defines his struggle to secure a safe environment for his young family. The owner builder has many choices in materials but this author fell back on his heritage to build a solid home of timber, slate and stone!

'Unwarranted Influence' were two pertinent words contained in President Eisenhower's departing speech in January 1961. Tom Law's latest book is about contemporary wars and the evil of the armaments industries where profit looms large over human lives. But mostly, it is about the urgent need to eliminate nuclear weapons. There have been many organisations across the world with the same intent but always to be frustrated by the superpowers and their generals! Tom is vehement in his argument that change will only come about by the dedicated application of international humanitarian law at the United Nations General Assembly. International law and a constant 'demand' by people is the best way forward to bring this goal to fruition. Time is short if humanity is to avert some final catastrophic conflict ending civilisation upon the planet.

By **Tom Law** ISBN 9780987629814

Tears from a Persian Rose by Tom Law

A short booklet on rules and values by which to guide one's life. A religious text that is general and not specifically belonging wholly to any of the major religions. Values that have been handed down over the millennia and consequently never changing in human civilisation.

ISBN 9780648226857

Helter Skelter ISBN 9780648226819

The title of 'Helter Skelter', Tom Law's book, almost speaks for itself. Basically, due to human folly, the writing leads us to the world's end with perhaps the survival of just a few reverting to a pre high tech existence. The storyline is interwoven with political outpourings, observations and graffiti ramblings. Sequence is a problem as factual narrative merges into drama, futuristic fantasy and prediction. So be warned: the flow is deceptive as the text is driven into cataracts, over waterfalls and through chasms lined with sharp rocks and oblique boulders. The writing is at times confused, abstract and didactic.. in other words, unconventional! Never the less, apart from being confronting it is a worthwhile read hopefully with lessons to be learned. Although the tome displays bucket loads of negativity and evil, the coda is a final escape route to the possibility of an alternative and possibly something better. Touches upon all the current problems and dilemmas facing humanity.

Love and Insults by Tom Law

Compendium of poems with some written and collected over many decades. However, the majority are of more recent ilk varying in texture, mode and triviality cum more serious. There is some romance, some politics and some appeal to the spiritual person with an admixture of material that some will find offensive- "it is a risk I must always follow!"

ISBN 9780648702726

amazon.com amazon.com.au amazon.co.uk amazon.de

longership.com

A MESSAGE FROM THE SMITH FAMILY CEO LISA O'BRIEN:

"We truly believe supporting a child's education is the best way to help break the cycle of disadvantage. By giving disadvantaged children and young people the support and resources they need to achieve their full potential, our impact will have a lasting effect on those we help today, and for generations to come.

The Smith Family
everyone's family

The Smith Family
everyone's family

Change the Course of a Child's Life !

https://www.thesmithfamily.com.au/
https://www.thesmithfamily.com.au/sponsor-a-child
https://www.thesmithfamily.com.au/donate

One in six Australian children and young people living in poverty need our support to make the most of their education. I urge you to explore our website to learn more about this important issue, our programs, and how you can make a difference."

1800 024 069

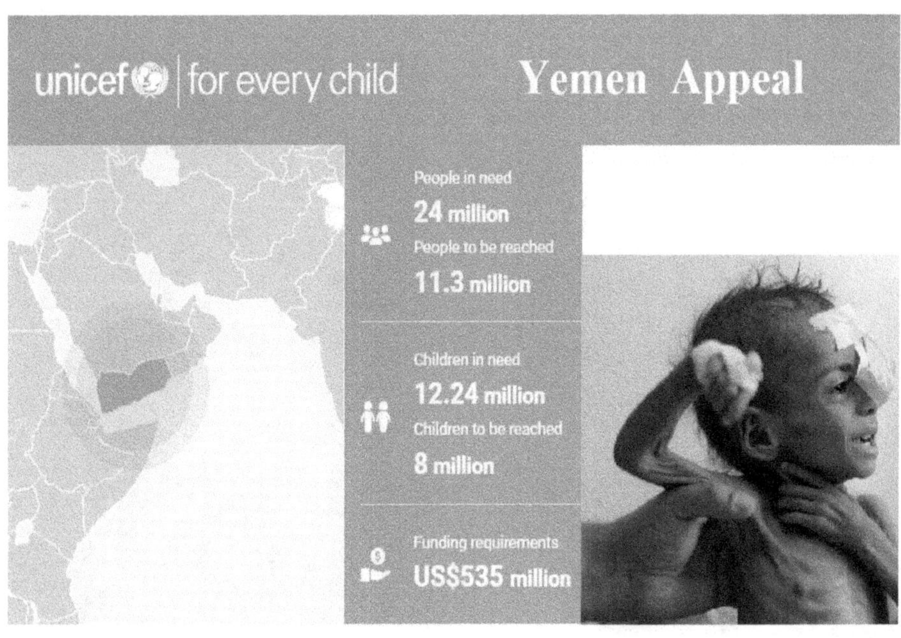

UN describes Yemen as: "the worst situation in the world !"

https://www.unicef.org.au/donate/donate-once

About the Author

Tom Law has lived on and off in East Gippsland, Victoria, Australia for a period of nigh on forty years. Originally from England, he was educated at Melbourne High School and later at Monash University. He describes his academic progress as chequered. "The problem with education is that it can get in the way of living…" But Tom never lets the dust settle under his feet and seriously views learning as his life-blood along with exploration of everything. As a teacher of chemistry he has worked in many different countries, Indonesia and China in particular. This story is purely fictional but has some elements of personal experiences of a small timber mill community of which he was a part for some twenty years. Building his life and home 'among the gum trees' he developed a deep affinity and love for the natural environment of this unique part of Australia. "Very few places experience the convergence of bird life from such a wide range of habitats… forest, high plains and coastal dwellers all breeze in and out of this area, depending on the season and prevailing weather. Migratory types such as swallows visit from as far away as China. When I first came here as a young man I could distinguish between a wattle tree and a eucalyptus but that is where it ended. Now I can view a Blackwood and differentiate it from a variety of these trees."

Tom built his first house from natural materials at hand… stone, timber, slate and whatever could be recycled from earlier building materials left over from the gold era of the mid-nineteenth century. "So many cultures have made an impact on this area in a brief frenetic period of gold mining. They came from China, Europe and North America in search of their fortunes. Some stayed, some died penniless and others returned home after some success. What now takes less than a two hour drive to a large regional town took three days at least by wagon and horse. The local cemetery tells tales of woe and grief from a bygone age of hardship and struggle difficult to comprehend in modern times."

Tom has two adult sons from his first marriage plus a daughter and son from his second marriage to an Indonesian lady.

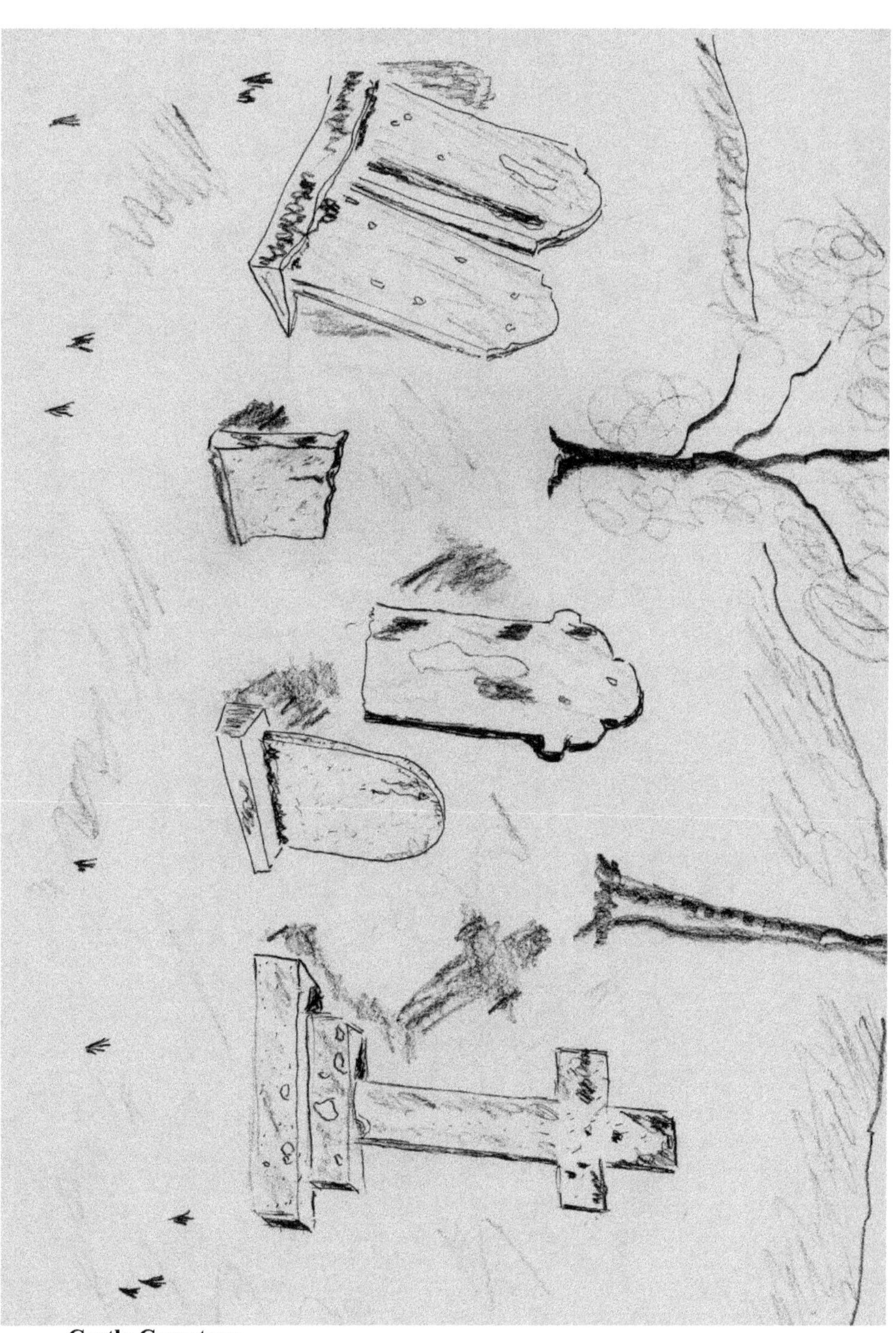

Castle Cemetery

Boy in Blue Raincoat is a short and simple story about a boy whose family roots can be traced back to the convict era. Growing up in Eastern Victoria, Australia, in a remote timber mill town in the nineteen sixties, the boy finds solace and joy in the natural environment away from the town. He is a loner, has few friends at school and despised a little by a minority of his teachers due to his father's prison record. Despite this, he has both a great appreciation and love for his dad. The boy finds unexpected true friendship with a Japanese soldier still in hiding from a distant war. Both the boy and the soldier must adjust to the intrusion of a new family into their favourite bush retreat. Also, the boy finds love from the daughter of a wealthy grazier; but just as things are looking up, his whole world is upturned by the unfolding of a train of events beyond his control.

Tom Law explores a brief window in time of the culture of a small remote rural community and its impact on the lives of outsiders that have chosen to join. An enjoyable read with sharpened insight into the continuing Australian theme of the collision between the settlers settled and the newcomers.

www.ingramcontent.com/pod-product-compliance
Lightning Source LLC
LaVergne TN
LVHW020637100826
845148LV00012B/2214